Alice A. Duchess of Buckingham & Chandos

Glimpses of Four Continents

Letters written during a tour in Australia, New Zealand, & North America, in 1893

Alice A. Duchess of Buckingham & Chandos

Glimpses of Four Continents
Letters written during a tour in Australia, New Zealand, & North America, in 1893

ISBN/EAN: 9783337192914

Printed in Europe, USA, Canada, Australia, Japan

Cover: Foto ©Andreas Hilbeck / pixelio.de

More available books at **www.hansebooks.com**

H. Buckingham and Chandos

GLIMPSES OF FOUR CONTINENTS: LETTERS WRITTEN DURING A TOUR IN AUSTRALIA, NEW ZEALAND, & NORTH AMERICA, IN 1893.

BY THE

DUCHESS OF BUCKINGHAM & CHANDOS

WITH PORTRAITS AND ILLUSTRATIONS
FROM THE AUTHOR'S SKETCHES, ETC.

> 'To a wise man all the world's a soil.
> It is not Italy, nor France, nor Europe
> That must bound me, if my fates call me forth.'
>
> *Ben Jonson.*

LONDON

JOHN MURRAY

NEW YORK

DODD MEAD AND COMPANY

1894

TO THE MEMORY

OF

MY HUSBAND

RICHARD PLANTAGENET

DUKE OF BUCKINGHAM AND CHANDOS

PREFACE

WHAT possessed you two to think of going to Australia? This question has been put to me and my cabin-mate so often that I almost feel as if we ought to apologise for having gone there and enjoyed ourselves so much. The idea of this journey had a very simple beginning, viz., seeing my cousin's wife making blue cotton pinafores for her little girl to wear on board ship, and talking of their voyage to New Zealand as others would talk of a trip to Paris. "You see," she said, "it does not seem so long as you suppose: first one stops at Gibraltar, then at Malta, Brindisi, Suez, Aden, and Ceylon; and the only long part is from Ceylon to Albany in King George's Sound, and that

is only ten days.   After reaching Australia,
one feels one has almost arrived at New
Zealand, although it is quite a little voyage
to get there from Melbourne."

A fortnight later I met my future
"cabin-mate" at a shooting-box in the
Highlands, and persuaded her relatives
that a sea voyage would be the best thing
in the world for her, and we wrote at once
for a three-berth cabin on the P. and O.
S. S. *Arcadia*, to sail on the 14th October.
I do not envy any one the week before
embarking, for the first time, on so long a
journey.   The rushing about in London
from shop to shop (greatly impeded by the
wet weather and yellow fogs), the ordering
summer garments, and trying to realise
how hot it will be in the Red Sea, produce
a certain confusion of mind ; and it is
just a mercy that, under the circumstances,
one gets anything like a suitable outfit for

the glorious winter of blue skies to which
one is hurrying. The difficulty of com-
pressing one's luggage is very great, as of
course one has to take many wraps and a
few warm dresses; besides, as we were going
to stay at various Government Houses
where there would probably be functions
of sorts, we had to lay in a certain quantity
of evening gowns, and also invest in
canvas-bags and cabin-boxes to fit under
our berths. People were most kind in
presenting us with a variety of things and
books they thought would be useful, and
against our better judgment we encumbered
ourselves with these "presents," only to
regret it when too late.

Board ship is not the place to read
improving books, and as to a tea-basket,
one has hardly energy to drink the tea
that is poured out, much less make it.
If you go to a picnic in Australia, you

make billy tea in a tin can as the "Sun-downers" do; and although it may be rather amusing to play your guitar on board ship, and sing to it with a good chorus in the Indian Ocean by starlight, it is a different matter when you come to cross the American continent, and there is no room for it in the cars, porter after porter having to be bribed to find a place for it where it would not get smashed ; so my advice is, "travel light."

Now that Hilda and I are fairly started I will begin to quote from my Journal, parts of which used to be sent home to go the round of the family.

LIST OF ILLUSTRATIONS

LETTER No. 1.

STEAM SHIP "ARCADIA,"
INDIAN OCEAN, *4th November* 1892.

WE left London on the 14th October at eleven o'clock from Liverpool Street Station. A sister, a niece, an uncle, two aunts, several cousins, and other friends came to see us off, and, as most of the other passengers were also liberally provided with belongings, the confusion was wonderful. However, at last we got safely into the saloon carriage of the right train to Tilbury Dock, where friends and all were packed like herrings in a barrel on a small tug to go out to the *Arcadia*.

Such a big ship she looked as we climbed up her side! and the first thing we noticed was the Lascars swarming about in their blue blouses, red turbans and sashes, and white trousers, with bare brown arms and feet. They looked very cold and miserable at the mouth of the Thames, but since we got into warm climates they are different beings.

My cook and housemaid asked leave to come and see me off at the ship, but they were so afraid of being left behind, that after a short inspection of the cabin, dining-saloon, and upper deck, they returned to the tug long before it was at all necessary.

No one who has not seen an enormous floating palace like this can form any idea how wonderful it is. Everything proceeds with the regularity of clockwork ; a bugle sounds for meals, and if any one is ill he can always have food brought to him in his cabin or on deck. There is a whole army of stewards in white trousers and blue jackets who wait at table. They are paid £12 for the trip, and of course get tips as well, as every one gives something to their table steward. Many youths are glad to engage themselves in this capacity as a means of getting out to the colonies.

For the first two days of the voyage it was very stormy, although the stewardess would not acknowledge there was even half a gale on. Strangely enough almost every one was sick ; and as I had got a slight chill on that horrid little tug, the doctor kept me in my berth. One begins to wonder, under these circumstances, what on earth induced one to cross the briny ocean, but of course one doesn't start fair on these occasions, for what with the packing and many good-byes one is fairly worn out.

The moment of the little tug's going back to shore carrying a sad-hearted crowd of friends and relations (half of them in tears) waving hats and handkerchiefs, and kissing their hands again and again, cannot fail to give the most determined and brave-hearted travellers lumps in their throats. We stood close together, and remarked how horrid this sort of thing was, and that we were glad we had not to go through it often, and how much worse it would be if this were a troopship and we soldiers going off to the wars. When the last little white rag had ceased waving, and the anxious faces were lost to sight, we descended to our cabin, and tried to impress on my maid that she had only two hours of calm sea to unpack and get things ship-shape.

At first it seemed perfectly hopeless to stow our manifold goods and chattels away, and my sketching things and paint-boxes always block up the road. Eventually we settled down, had a pretty good dinner, and sat on deck, as we steamed down the river, till quite late. It was a trial for two such tall people to get used to undressing in so small a room. Dressing was not so bad, as one could remain in her berth till the other was out of the way.

Three days later we began to enjoy life ; and it was a most pleasurable sensation to recline, well wrapped up, on our deck chairs, a bright sun overhead, and the ship flying along through the blue waves.

The cabins are very well ventilated, so much so that you can hear pretty distinctly everything that goes on next door.   There was a poor little baby that constantly cried, and its cheerful young nurse, who sang, " Ta-ra-ra-boom-daye," " Mrs. Enry Awkins is a first-class Name," and other, too well-known, tunes, till we could have strangled her with pleasure.   I have heard of people on land being very much annoyed by the noises of their neighbours, and many pretty village quarrels which have resulted from the said noises ; but if people are incon-siderate in that respect on board ship, one has to grin and bear it, as there is no escape.   Then, perhaps, there is some one with a bad cough, or a man who whistles out of tune all the time he is dressing, and then comes thundering down the pass-age, and breaks his shins over your hot

water can and swears dreadfully. When
he is gone a young lady peeps out and re-
marks in a cheerful voice, on finding the
offending can, "Oh, this is what caused
all the damnation," upon which muffled
guffaws are heard from a neighbouring
cabin.

There are a lot of children on board
who get rather troublesome and cross with
the heat, and run about playing at hide-
and-seek amongst the deck chairs. Everybody almost has a deck chair, and when
one is sitting in it, that is the only place
one can call one's own.

The cabins are all painted white, and
have folding-up washing-stands, and rows
of hooks to hang things on, and we had
large cretonne bags made with lots of
pockets to stuff shoes, etc. in. Above
our heads is a sort of arrangement which
one sees in a dairy for cheeses ; this holds

our hats and parasols.   Under the berths there is room for a cabin-box ; and once a week, on baggage day, passengers are allowed to get up boxes from the baggage-room.

One night I was just going to bed when a large black rat came into my cabin, and began to hop about all over my things : the rats come up from the hold, but do not often attack ladies in their cabins.   I was dreadfully frightened by this unwelcome visitor, but refrained from screaming, as I fled down the passage in my nightdress, and got into a neigh-bour's room ; then I sent for a steward, who found a hole in the floor, which he stuffed up with a towel, and mended next morning with a piece of tin.

My maid was still more unfortunate, as her rat went up her petticoats, and nearly gave her a fit.   She said it was as large as a rabbit! In the second class, one woman found her baby being devoured in its berth, and actually the horrid rat was hanging on to its lip.

There was also a parachute lady who was attacked by one, and her screams were so loud that some of us thought the ship was on fire; considering in what a dangerous way she made her living, one would not have expected her to be so much affected by such a trifle as a rat. They say these animals come to the cabins to look for water as, like other folk, they suffer from thirst in the tropics.

After that I used to put my sketching-board across the doorway, in hopes that, when the rats found this slight obstacle, they would turn into my neighbour's cabin for a drink. A short poem soon went the round of the ship, entitled, "The Rat and the Duchess."

The first place we stopped at was Gibraltar, and most delighted we were to get on shore, and drive in a rickety little trap through the fortifications and up to the market, where we bought some bunches of roses, heliotrope, and verbena, and a large grass bag full of grapes, figs, and apples, for about one shilling and sixpence. On the other side was the meat market, and then the Moor market, where stately Arabs, in long white garments, sold plucked fowls and live turkeys—such beautiful birds, copper coloured and white. I longed to buy one, but Hilda suggested it would be a troublesome pet in our small cabin !

We saw some English soldiers belonging to a Highland regiment, so smart in their kilts and pith helmets ; and further on, where the Spanish lines begin, were some Spanish soldiers. We also met some huntsmen exercising a pack of hounds. The officers hunt a good deal.

After two hours we returned to the *Arcadia*.

On Friday, 21st October, we reached Malta, where we were met and taken on shore by a young cousin (Hon. Edward Murray) in the Cameron Highlanders, who arrived in a small green boat like a gondola. We managed to make the most of our day on shore, and saw a great deal in a short time, in spite of a hot wind blowing the whole time, making everybody sticky and uncomfortable. We began by walking up a great many stone stairs leading from the harbour, and got desperately hot, as on board ship one becomes so out of condition for walking.

At last we were in the principal street of the town, full of shops, where we invested in a few necessaries, and then proceeded to turn in at the iron gates of the old palace of the Knights of St. John of Jerusalem, now used as the residence of the English Governor. We visited the armoury there, full of all sorts of curious helmets and coats of mail, swords, pikes, flint guns, and one huge suit of armour that belonged in former days to a giant who was more than seven feet high. His helmet was so heavy that we could hardly lift it, and we could not imagine any mortal supporting such a weight of metal. Afterwards we saw the Council chamber, all hung with valuable tapestry, and the reception-room, which reminded me of the state drawing-room at Stowe, the walls were covered with the same crimson brocade and heaps of old pictures.

After this we went across the square to the guard-room, where the young officers have to spend so much time in turns, liable to be called out at any moment of the day or night, so when they are on guard there they have to be very much on the alert. The white-washed walls are all decorated with their drawings and sketches, chiefly caricatures. My youngest brother was at one time stationed there, and contributed to the frescoes, so of course I looked at the place with great interest.

We now proceeded to hire a carriage and pair of white Arab horses, with long manes and tails, and after some bargaining, the driver agreed to take us for a fair sum to Citta Vecchia, where my cousin's camp was. It is about six or seven miles distant, past many detached houses and through little fields, from which the stones have gradually been cleared and built into walls, so that from a distance you cannot see the grass or vines in these little vineyards, and the country looks like a stony desert. The camp was at the top of a hill, and the mess-room, where we lunched, in a small villa, with a lovely view right across country to the blue sea. The food was black with flies, but we were very hungry, and the officers had done their best for us, so we did full justice to the repast.

After a short rest we walked to the Cathedral. Of course we were followed by a crowd of beggars, but we adopted the plan of hiring one boy to keep all the others off, and this succeeded admirably. The high altar was a wonderful sight, all inlaid with blue lapis lazuli, and covered with most beautiful tall candlesticks and much plate in solid silver. My cousin then took us to see his tent, pitched under some trees, and his beloved bulldog called Jack, a most formidable-looking animal, who soon made friends with us. In the middle of the tent was a little iron bedstead, with mosquito curtains coming down all round to keep off " the buzzing night-flies, who hush you to your slumber."

Our return journey was made in a small tram railway, very like the one from Quainton Road to Wotton. It seemed quite like an old friend to see the little engine panting and snorting, but, oh! it was hot in that tram car, and we got a good jolting ; however, it only took half-an-hour getting back.

We were to have gone to see the polo ponies, but were too exhausted to walk about, and were thankful to reach the comparative coolness of the Cathedral Church of St. John, where vespers were going on. The scene was most picturesque and very solemn.

All the women in Malta wear black, and

a sort of black silk hood and veil. This costume was adopted by order of the Pope when, in 1798, the town surrendered to Bonaparte, and received a French garrison. It was afterwards blockaded by a British squadron, was forced to surrender through famine in 1800, and by the Treaty of Paris in 1814, was confirmed to Great Britain. It seems rather hard that the ladies should be doomed to perpetual mourning for a calamity which no longer exists.

By this time it was five o'clock, and we were glad to accept a kind invitation from the flag lieutenant and his charming wife, who had been our fellow-passengers, to rest and dine at their house, from which there was a beautiful bird's-eye view of the harbour. We sat on the balcony in a complete draught, trying to get cool, and drinking excellent tea, and watching a Dutch vessel come in and begin coaling. It was nice to get into a large airy bedroom, have a good wash, and be able to stretch about without fear of up-setting some one or something. We sent to the ship for our evening dresses, and had a very pleasant ending to our long day ashore. Our young hostess wished she had had more time to unpack ; but, need-less to say, we noticed no deficiencies, her Maltese servants having done their utmost to make the rooms look smart and pretty before her arrival. Alas ! our return to the ship was not so enjoyable, a smell of coal dust everywhere, all the port-holes shut ; and very soon the decks were a sheet of water, all the black men washing them down as fast as they could. At 12 P.M. we were rudely awakened from our first sleep by the noise of the anchor chains being wound up, and the shouting of the

Lascars. Our next port was Brindisi, which we reached on Sunday, 23rd. Service in the saloon at eleven o'clock.

There was not so much to see as at Malta, but every one was again enchanted to go on shore. We landed at 3 P.M. and walked about the steep stony streets, and up to a curious Roman pillar, which used to be the end of the Appian Way. This town was the ancient Brundusium, and was the place whence the Roman generals almost invariably sailed in their wars with Greece, Macedonia, and Asia. In consequence of its situation, it has been the scene of many historical events. Virgil died there. Horace in one of his satires has immortalised it. Agrippina landed on its shore with the ashes of Germanicus. On the fall of the Roman Empire it shared in the general calamities which befell Roman cities.

We looked into several ancient churches, in one of which were a number of life-sized figures of saints ; one of them in a long red cloak, on a gray horse, that looked like a rocking - horse, and St. Theresa in a nun's habit, in a glass case. One could hardly imagine people feeling very reverent when praying before them. Mustering our best Italian we hired a funny little carriage, and drove out of the town past the old fortress-prison guarded by Italian soldiers in their light-blue uniforms.

The mass of masonry, lit up by the afternoon sun, looked most picturesque, all reflected in the water, as we drove further round the bay ; but we could not help thinking how many sad and weary prisoners had been incarcerated within its walls, not for a few weeks or days, but for years and years, in the horrible dungeons.

Hilda produced her kodak and did several small photos of this interesting fortress.

We continued our drive till we reached a bright salmon-coloured villa, belonging to the Turkish Consulate, surrounded by a pretty terraced garden with steps down to the water, and flower-beds. On the other side was a vineyard, where the vine leaves were all turning brown and red, with the grapes hanging in tempting clusters. The gardener proceeded to invite us to rest ourselves on two garden seats, while he fetched a large china dessert - basket piled with the delicious fruit; also a bottle of sweet wine made from the grapes of the vineyard, chattering to us all the time in Italian. There was a splendid old pine-tree under which we sat, and the relief of getting away from the noisy harbour and all the crowds of people on board was very great. Some blind musicians came in a boat and played several airs on their mandolines. One called "Spingola Francese" Hilda used to sing to her guitar. It is really only a little song of a street seller asking if you will buy his French pins. Not very romantic when you come to dissect it.

They also sang "Santa Lucia," and the bull-fight march out of "Carmen." The gardener and the pine-tree had their photos taken. At first he would not turn towards us except in crab-like fashion, and we thought he did not approve of our proceedings; but it turned out that he had been badly stung on the eye, and was afraid he would not come out handsome enough. We had a good laugh over this.

On our way back to the ship we passed the market-place, where there was a crowd of swarthy people selling fruit of all kinds, and making a great deal of noise. Lots of our Lascars mingled with the crowd, buying mangoes, melons, and figs.

Almost every one now wears white dresses and shady hats, and we rejoice in brilliant sunshine all day long. We had a concert on board the other night, and everybody who could sing, including the captain, had to perform. We sit out on deck in thin dresses till eleven o'clock at night, and some of the men sleep on deck.

Yesterday there was an eclipse of the moon, very interesting to watch. In England something always happens to prevent one seeing it, either a fog or much rain.

We have had several tropical showers the last day or two; they do not last long, but make the deck and awnings, under which our rows of deck chairs are placed, all wet and dripping. Then there is a stampede, everybody dragging their chairs under cover ; and the black fellows come round with mops and pails, and swish the water all along the scuppers.

28th October.—We reached Port Said at four o'clock. All the Lascars were massed forward, and with a brilliant sunset reflected on them made a gorgeous picture. There was much delay about landing caused by the search for a man, who was "wanted" by the police, among the second-class passengers. We were told that he was a most agreeable person, and used to keep his shipmates in roars of laughter. He was travelling with a young wife and baby, and excited no suspicion that he was a forger, or something of that sort.

At last we got on shore, too late for a

donkey-ride in the desert, on which Hilda had set her heart. It would have been most unsafe to go even a few yards down any of the side streets. The population consists chiefly of scoundrels of all countries.

The shops were brilliantly lighted, and as we passed along, escorted by some of our fellow-travellers, touts rushed out on us with red fezes on their heads, and in voluble pigeon English invited us to enter, each declaring that we would not find anything so good, so beautiful, or so cheap, as at his store. "You come in, missey ; you look round ; plenty you want —very cheap, sar. You not oblige buy ; you step in." The embroidered jackets and caps found many purchasers, and we invested in various fans and some sweet-meats, lumps of Turkish delight, and chocolate drops. We procured, too, some pineapple ices in a café, which tasted perfectly excellent after the heat and struggle of landing in open boats from the ship, rowed by cursing crews of savage-looking Arabs, jostling each other's boats and using awful language, if we could have understood it. The street was a wide road of dirty, black sand with no side-walk, and one sank into unsuspected holes in walking up from the landing-place.

Before we left the *Arcadia* the coal barges had reached her side, and were swarming with what looked, in the flaring glare of swinging coal fires, like an army of industrious black devils, all rushing up and down the gangways with burdens of coal on their heads, and chanting a sort of dirge at the top of their voices. It was a very curious scene, all by moonlight, surrounded by other vessels covered with lights and red, blue, and green lamps.

27th October.—We woke up to find ourselves in the Suez Canal, desert sands on each side, and very wild-looking Arabs roaming along the shore in loose cotton garments, rather like a surplice, which they speedily tucked up or took off altogether if any one responded to their wild cries by throwing a small coin into the water for them to dive for.

Some Arab traders hooked their boat on to us, and climbed with the agility of cats on board with green oranges to sell. They were dressed in a variety of coloured garments like a long coat to the heels, and white baggy trousers and turbans, and when they were not swinging themselves on deck by a rope looked very grave and dignified. We saw our first camel in the distance, and felt we had really got to Eastern countries. Several ships passed us in the Canal, one with a lot of Chinamen on board, but an English captain and officers. Another was a German boat, but she looked very dirty; in fact they all did, as they were only traders.

1st November.—We reached Aden at about nine o'clock A.M. Then an extraordinary scene began. The vessel was surrounded by a screaming crowd of Arab youths, who came off from the shore in all sorts of small craft, some in clumsy boats painted red and green, others in little canoes scooped out of a tree, which they kept constantly baling by splashing the water out with their hands and feet.

The decks began to swarm with traders selling long, twisted, polished horns and many-coloured baskets in the form of gourds, and pieces of silk and cotton, scarves and handkerchiefs, and ostrich feathers and boas—asking far more than they meant to take, and cheating everybody in every possible way, measuring the yards of stuff wrong, and acting in a truly Eastern fashion. Some of them were Jews, with black ringlets on each side of their faces (the rest of their heads being shaved), and long black robes over coloured ones ; others were Armenians, in pink and canary-coloured garments ; others negroes quite black, all their gaudy costumes and orange-coloured and ebony faces glistening in the sun. It was a perfect pandemonium all day long; the Arab boys never seemed to tire of shouting, " Hab a dive, sar," meaning we were to throw them sixpences, which they dived for very cleverly.

We were rowed ashore in an Arab boat by the wildest set of figures you can imagine ; one of them with a coal black face and bright yellow hair, like orange tow, sticking up in tufts all over his head.

I began to sketch him from my end of the boat, upon which he made some grimaces of high disapproval, and producing a large, gaudy, crimson silk handkerchief he proceeded to envelop his head in it, holding the ends in his teeth while he continued rowing. As the sun was pouring down, and the reflection from the waves very dazzling, we felt quite sorry that he should think it necessary to wrap himself up. I believe he must have been a Mussalman, as it is against their religion to have any image made of man, who is the image of God. A mischievous little Arab, who was steersman, chattered the whole half-hour it took to row ashore, chiefly on his extreme desire that " Missee should give him a backsheesh."

On landing we were beset by a troop of drivers offering their carriages for hire. We selected two for our party, and were soon galloping along the road to the tanks, about five miles from the port, through a gateway and road cut in the rocks. We passed several caravan camels with different burdens ; one was a moving mass of dry sticks, like an animated underwood ; some were muzzled, as they were addicted to biting passers-by.

We passed the Arab cemetery, a desert of rock and stone slabs, with no wall round it ; then entered the old Arab town, where we saw a delightful little light brown Arab baby with a string of blue beads round its waist, and long gold ear-rings ; women in gaudy garments, some part of which was wound round their heads. The whole population seem to live in a sort of open room on the shady side of their houses, sitting or lying on rude chairs or benches. Little boys, with a waistcloth for sole garment, followed the carriages and crowded round us when we alighted, begging, and saying they were orphans—" No fadar, sar." " No moodder, missey "—to excite our compassion. I must say, if they were orphans they were very well fed ones.

The walk through the garden to the tanks was exceedingly hot, in fact the rocks formed a sort of sun-trap, and reflected light and heat from every corner of their surface. We were thankful for our double shady hats and double-lined parasols. A guide accompanied us in a white dress and purple turban. These tanks are like a small quarry in the rocks, date from very ancient times, and are said to have been made by King Solomon and utilised by the Romans. There was a view of the town and the sea beyond, which I sketched while the others went on to the second tank.

The ship has been rolling all morning, and the heat is fearful. We expect to get to Colombo to-day about four o'clock and sleep on shore, Sir William and Lady Clark having invited us to be their guests at the hotel—a great treat, if we are not eaten up by mosquitoes.

On Saturday, 5th November, we had a fancy dress dance on board. The Lascars decorated the deck with a variety of flags and bunting, and all the ladies concocted dresses for themselves. I appeared as Katharine of Aragon; and Hilda, as a vivandière, had a *succès fou* wearing the cap and jacket she bought at Port Said, and carrying a small glass barrel, painted blue and white by the carpenter.

GIBRALTAR.

MOUNTAINS NEAR ADEN.

LETTER No. 2.

S.S. " ARCADIA,"
SOUTHERN OCEAN, 14th November 1892.

IN my last letter I believe we had got as far as Aden. You have no idea how hazy one becomes at sea as to time and dates. For one thing one's watch is perpetually wrong, as they change the clocks every day to get them right by Australian time when we reach that far-off country.

The next excitement of the voyage was arriving at Colombo on 6th November.

After being pent up in a ship like a flock of sheep, everybody feels in a most restless state.   As soon as we get in sight of land, all crowd on the bows of the vessel, and spyglasses are produced and passed from one to another in order that we may feast our eyes on houses and green trees.   We also watched the surf breaking on the shore in showers of spray.   Beyond was a fringe of tall palm-trees, and before we reached the lighthouse and harbour we could see the dim outline of the mountain range.

The weather had been showery, and we were afraid of a ducking, as the sky was lowering. The sun went down, and before we were allowed to land it was quite dark. I cannot describe the scene of confusion. Many of the passengers were going off to the *Sutlej*, which started the following day for Hong Kong. Some of them had babies and very small children, who cried from fright and fatigue. Piles of luggage had been hauled up from the hold by the Lascars.

The ship was surrounded by steam-tugs and row-boats filled with shrieking Arabs. Everybody wished to go on shore at once, and the gangway was blocked by a struggling crowd, who got wedged together with their large bags and baskets which they carried in their hands.

When our turn did come to climb down the slippery steps over the ship's side, we felt as if we should hardly arrive alive out of the hubbub. Long black arms stretched out from the darkness and hauled us on board, and stuffed us into the stifling little cabin of the steam-tug, illuminated by a flickering lantern.

One unfortunate passenger, in trying to help a charming old lady and hold his bag at the same time, missed his footing and

went right down into the black water, bag
and all.   He had just sense to let go the
bag, and fortunately came up at the same
spot, and was pulled out with no further
damage than a sprained shoulder ; but he
looked rather ill and shaken for some days
after his ducking.   His young wife, fortunately, did not hear of the accident till
she met him safe, but dripping, at the
hotel.   Everybody got separated in the
crush.

We had not gone far from the ship
when our tug was very nearly swamped,
as we collided with a coal barge.   All
were bumped out of their seats, and the
shrieks and yells from the Arabs and
Singalese oarsmen were terrific.   In their
hurry to back off the barge, they got our
tug in the way of a big vessel, and those
who were on the deck thought our last
hour was come, and that we should have

to plunge into the black waters, at the risk of being hit on the head by one of the numerous long oars plying in all directions. One girl fainted, and if her mother had not caught her, would have fallen into the sea. Another got hauled up in a rope attached to the machinery, and was nearly strangled ; her shrieks added to the general row. Mercifully we just escaped by the skin of our teeth, as the saying is, but it was a narrow shave ; we did not understand how narrow till we got on shore.

A few steps from the landing we reached the hotel, nearly run over several times by erratic fly-drivers, all cracking their whips and screaming at the top of their voices We felt dazed after an experience of this kind, and all collapsed quite exhausted into some cane chairs that were in the veranda of the hotel, for although pitch dark, it was extremely hot.

Beyond the veranda was a huge dining-room, with a polished floor and scarlet and white punkahs waving overhead. I could only just stand upright under them. Hurrying about in all directions were the native servants, such clever, handy waiters, dressed in white coats and trousers, with scarlet sashes. They had most intelligent faces, very dark brown, and jet black hair done up in a little knob behind, and surmounted by a smart smoking-cap in coloured embroidery; some of the men wore beautiful tortoise-shell combs.

We thought the dinner excellent, and admired the beautiful flowers on the table, such as one only sees in conservatories at home.

After dinner we walked in the bazaar, where the native shopkeepers did their best to tempt every one with their wares.

Some were jewellers', full of precious stones, sapphires, amethysts, Indian garnets and moon-stones, and silver ornaments, spoons, and bowls, and wonderful embossed trays, silver on copper, of all shapes and sizes. There were also toy bullock-carts for children, and ivory elephants and Indian shawls, and silks of all descriptions. The shopkeepers dressed in a variety of costumes, according as they were Mohammedans, Buddhists, or Hindus. The Hindus in many cases had a round mark the size of a sixpence on their foreheads, made with white ashes — a sign that they had been sealed by the priest at their temple, when they went to perform their devotions.

We slept in bare rooms, so cool and delicious after the hot cabins : mosquito net curtains all round the beds, and the windows opening wide on to a balcony covered in with fine matting to keep out the insects. The native servants kept up a constant chattering till well on into the night. We looked into a garden where, as soon as it was light, various dusky figures began to move about among the strange trees and plants. I saw a figure, that I took for a woman, combing its long black hair over its face, but when it whisked it up in a knot behind, I saw it was one of the bearded waiters: his long white skirt completed the illusion.

We could hardly eat our breakfast for longing to begin sight-seeing. An Indian conjurer was performing in the veranda, and I recognised all the tricks, that I had so often heard described by the Duke and my step-daughter as having been seen by them in India. He carried a cobra serpent in a basket, and eventually twisted it round his neck. A crowd of Singalese gathered round, watching with pleased, amused faces a performance they must have seen scores and scores of times, just as the little street boys, and big boys too, watch a performance of Punch at home.

My London housemaid told me that her little boy would follow a Punch man for miles, and had once or twice got lost and been brought home by the police. He was only four years old, and amused them very much at the police station by dancing and singing on the table; but when they wanted to put him to sleep there, wrapped up in the tablecloth, he said, No, he could not sleep in a table-cloth, but wanted to go and find his own little mother.

After the conjurer had taken his de-parture, we proceeded for a long drive to a place called Mount Lavinia. Our way lay through the native town, which was very interesting, such wonderfully picturesque groups of black, brown, and yellow people of all sizes, ages, and occupations. Again we saw dear, fat, sleek, brown babies, just able to toddle, with their strings of beads round their waists, and beautiful little children, with lovely dark eyes, sitting in groups at every cottage door, just as they do at home.

The first place we stopped at was a Buddhist temple—our guide belonged to that religion, took great pride in showing us all the curious paintings; and there were all the priests, with shaven heads and bright saffron-coloured robes and bare arms and feet. A huge image of Buddha, whom they speak of as " Our Lord," in a recumbent posture, had wonderful green eyes, which they said were made of emeralds. There were two other images of him standing and sitting. All the walls were covered with pictures of his history—how he had a mysterious call to separate himself from the rest of mankind, and left his wife and child; and how gold-coloured robes were given him, and he founded the priesthood. There were also fearful pictures of the different hells that people will go to who break the commandments, which seem to be something the same as ours— thou shalt not steal; honour to parents, etc. On the ceiling were painted the signs of the zodiac and the seven planets.

One pagoda-sort of temple in the grounds was said to be too holy for us to see. The images of Buddha were very gaudily painted, and enclosed by glass doors, rather like a big cupboard—I suppose in case we unbelievers should be tempted to steal his eyes, or anything else. We were given some of the flowers that had been offered that morning.

Hilda took a photograph of the oldest priest, and also one of the keeper of the temple and his children, who were delighted. The keeper showed us their sacred book. It was all written out in Singalese characters on strips of palm leaf about three feet long, and bound together with silver and crimson cords ; the leaves smelt very sweet.

We were followed from the temple back to our carriage by a crowd of children, all wanting to sell flowers or a strip of palm leaf writing. Our guide next took us to see a native house. It was a thatched cottage, very dark to keep out the sun, most clean and neat: modern conveniences, such as a paraffin lamp and a blue and white Manchester tablecover, looked rather out of place; also rather common chairs, with turkey-red seats. They showed us all their cooking pots, of strange shapes, and behind the house a fire on the ground with just a few bricks to keep it together, and a sort of frying-pan on it. They do not eat meat, as it is unlawful for them to take life, but subsist chiefly on rice and breadfruit. They seem to thrive on the diet, and their brown skins are well filled out, and shine in the sun. One girl spoke a word or two of English; she had large gold ear-rings and a striped garment wound gracefully round her.

One of the youngsters swarmed up a palm-tree in front of the cottage and brought down a couple of cocoa-nuts. A knife was produced, one end sliced off, and the milk of the cocoa-nut tilted into a glass for us to drink. If you put a little sugar into a tumbler of water and then steep a bit of apple in it, you will know what it is like,—rather nasty, I thought, but no doubt if one had passed several days in a tropical sun, in an open boat, previous to being wrecked on a desert island, one would then think such a beverage quite delicious.

After thanking the Singalese women, and presenting them with a rupee, we continued our drive ; and after going altogether for about six miles, we reached Mount Lavinia.

An hotel is built on an eminence looking over the sea, and lots of surf boats, called catamarans, were fishing and constantly coming ashore.   It was most amusing to watch them dash through the breakers. We walked to the beach, where rows of them were high and dry.   Swarms of little woolly - headed and straight - haired

urchins were clamouring to be allowed to climb a palm-tree, so we threw a small coin amongst them, and the scrimmage was tremendous.

Hilda took a kodak of it, and one of our fellow-passengers attempting to defend himself with his umbrella, and nearly lifted off his feet by the surging mass of little brown bodies. We saw some English soldiers quartered there who said they belonged to the Warwickshire Regiment. They wore topees to keep off the sun, and a sort of brown canvas clothes, very unlike the smart red coats at home. The conjurer had preceded us, and was again at his tricks before an admiring audience.

We returned to Colombo for lunch and found two other conjurers, very smart young fellows, with much larger and fatter serpents, performing in the veranda. There was, however, no time to admire them, as we were bent on having a turn in rickshaws before it was time to leave for the ship. Rickshaws are little hooded carriages, with long shafts, to hold one person only, drawn by a man who runs in the shafts quite as fast as a pony. Three of us raced through the streets in fits of laughter at the novelty of our drive.

About four o'clock we returned to our ship in the harbour-master's boat, rowed by Arabs in white garments and red turbans. This time we arrived without accident. The decks were crowded with traders worrying one out of one's life to buy their precious stones and bits of stuffs and silks. We were glad when the bell rang and they all went ashore.

The journey since leaving Ceylon has

been rather trying, as we have had rough weather and heavy seas. Many people were unable to leave their cabins, and very sick from the tossing and pitching. Even if we do feel ill in the morning, we always dress and come on deck, as our cabin is so far forward that one gets knocked about; and at night the noise of the creaking of the masts and the swishing of the water is deafening. One huge wave broke into the bathroom and flooded our passage.

The worst of rough weather is that the carpenter comes round and screws down all the port-holes, and one feels like a rat in a trap, and nearly suffocated for want of air. However, it is wonderful we manage to sleep so soundly. In the morning one feels stiff and sore, as if one had been beaten all over. It is now much cooler, and we begin to pack our cotton dresses and get out woollen ones on baggage day.

Letters will be posted to-morrow at King George's Sound, and we ought to write Christmas letters full of good wishes; but it is difficult to realise that you are all in the middle of winter at home.

You have no idea how curious it is to be in what they call a heavy sea, with perhaps a brilliant sun overhead, and the waves the colour of turquoise and sapphires. You see small mountains stretching as far as eye can reach, and you gradually get to the top of one, and down into a valley; then up again with a great deal of creaking and straining of timber and ropes—people all looking very drunk on deck, and trying to walk straight, but sent flying into each other's arms when they least expect it; profuse apologies; " Oh !

don't mention it." "Where are you trying to go to?" says some gentleman, seeing a lady struggling with her deck chair, and trying to drag it to a more sheltered position—"allow me"; he seizes on it, lurches up against a small table, where some one is working; off flies the workbox, reels of cotton into the scuppers; an unruly child comes past with its nurse after it, catches in a rope, and down it goes: such a yell. Or perhaps you are having your lunch on deck, and a gust of wind sends your glass of wine into your plate, and blows the fried potatoes all over the deck. In the second-class dining-room yesterday one poor lady got the whole cruet-stand into her lap by a sudden lurch of the ship. Sometimes a good deal of crockery is broken in this way. I saw them getting out the fiddles this morning; these are squares of wood to keep the bottles and things on the table, and look like little sheep-pens. I will send another letter from Melbourne.

P.S.—A happy Christmas and a good New Year.

A BUDDHIST PRIEST.

LETTER No. 3.

S.S. "ARCADIA,"
GREAT AUSTRALIAN BIGHT,
Saturday, 19th Nov. 1892.

SINCE leaving Colombo we have had some very rough weather, and it is a long voyage without a break. One begins to feel that one can hardly endure to remain on board ship another hour, or another minute. One begins to think of lions at the Zoo, and poor wild larks in small cages, and to have pity for all prisoners, whether animals, birds, or men.

The little people are the only ones who never seem to tire of the voyage, as running about the decks all day long is quite enough exercise for their small legs.   My little cousin, Mary, was indefatigable as an organiser of games ; and sometimes she would collect her playfellows round my chair, and we would tell each other stories, or play at dreams, each one relating in turn his supposed experiences in the land of Nod, while the others had to guess what scene in Bible or secular history he was trying to set forth.   The children did it perfectly gravely, but I used to have some trouble to conceal my laughter.

Sometimes one came across an amusing scene on deck ; for instance — one stout old gentleman fell asleep in his deck chair, and in the one next to him a large wax doll had been put to bed by its little mistress : gradually the sun came round, and they both began to melt, and did look so absurd, side by side, with glistening countenances and very red cheeks.

At last we reached the harbour of King George's Sound. Early in the morning on the 17th we wake up in a calm bay, surrounded by low hills covered with scrub, and see the small town of Albany glittering in the sunshine. Alas! we hear some very sad news ; the engineer who attends to the refrigerating chamber, had fallen down into it the night before and broken his neck. The poor fellow was just going down to get himself a glass of iced water before going to bed, and the vessel gave a greater roll than usual. He did not fall above ten feet, but landed on the back of his head against an iron ladder. He was only about thirty, and left a young wife. This sad occurrence cast a gloom over what would have been a very pleasant day. We all went ashore in a steam-tug, which took twenty minutes to reach the landing-place, and then we wandered down the only street of the town, and beyond into the country, where we saw a beautiful view of blue mountain ranges, thirty miles off, and gathered a quantity of wild flowers ; lots of geraniums, and tall Arum lilies growing like weeds. We could spare only two hours, which passed like lightning, and then we had all to crowd on the little tug again.

When we had disembarked or rather re-embarked, a sad procession carried the coffin of the engineer, covered with a Union Jack and a cross of the white lilies. All heads were uncovered, and the coffin placed on board the tug to be taken ashore for burial. It may be some little comfort for the poor wife to know that her husband was not buried at sea.

The climate at Albany is extremely

good for invalids, as it does not vary much
all the year round, and the soil is so dry.
It would be a very dull place to live in at
present, and a good hotel is much wanted.
The country round is very barren, and
grows nothing but scrub. We saw one or
two old natives in the town : every one
calls them Johnnie, and they were clothed
in coarse working clothes and slouch hats,
and very, very ugly, reminding one of scare-
crow figures of old rag-pickers in London.
But I afterwards bought some photos of
fine-looking fellows in native undress from
Queensland.

We had a little entertainment on board,
consisting of an exhibition of Mrs. Jarley's
Waxworks. They were most successful,
which was mainly due to the handsome
young lady who transformed herself into
the voluble Mrs. Jarley, with a powdered
wig and many wrinkles. Afterwards we

had singing and a supper party by special permission of the captain, who was unfortunately laid up with a bad cold, but ill or well, would have to turn out on the bridge when we made the Narrows. We all got rather reckless, and ended with a mad polka, which I played for till the stewards turned off the electric light. A short pillow fight ensued on the companion ; luckily I just escaped to bed before the first officer in a rage appeared on the scene to quell the rioters.

The near prospect of reaching land had been too much for us.

We left Albany in a gale of wind, but, fortunately, it was in our favour. I never saw anything so grand as the waves. There was a bright sun most of the time, and the whole sea a mass of foam. The distant view looked like jagged mountain ranges. Standing on the bows, holding one's hat on with one hand, and clutching the rails tight with the other, one could look over and see the vessel bound right out of the water, and then crash down through a big billow. The waves came in constant succession, like wild horses, their white manes flying in the breeze ; and the colours the water took were most beautiful, like all sorts of precious stones.   Occasionally a small rainbow appeared for a moment and sank into the sea.   Many albatrosses hovered round the track which we made in the waters, and which looked like a long blue serpent of a river in the wake of the ship --bright turquoise colour.

A fellow-passenger told me he had had to go in the teeth of a similar gale in the opposite direction, when his ship took five days from Adelaide to King George's Sound, the decks being under water all the time, and the passengers obliged to remain down below. To-day the sea has somewhat quieted down, and nobody seems to mind its vagaries much, as they have all got their sea-legs, although falls are frequent. My maid had a bad one yesterday, and had to go to bed, and get a lotion from the doctor, as she was much bruised; but it was very lucky, from the way she fell, that she did not go overboard.

Monday, 21st November.

Early yesterday morning we reached Port Adelaide. Everybody was up and dressed, and had breakfasted long before it was time to go on shore; but you require to be boxed up on board ship to understand the real pleasure of dry land! Lord Kintore, who is Governor there, sent an aide-de-camp in a steam-launch to fetch us

THE EARL OF KINTORE.   *To face p.* 61.

to the jetty, which is about a quarter of a mile long, a hot walk in a broiling sun, to the hotel, where we waited nearly an hour till the mail train (which did not hurry itself, and was engaged in digesting piles and piles of luggage) was ready to take us up to Adelaide. We employed the time in resting in a cool room, and refreshing ourselves with a drink of milk, and nice bread that wasn't sour.

We took half an hour to get up to the town, the train going calmly through the streets, ringing a bell to make people get out of the way. There we were met by the Governor, who proposed to drive us thirteen miles up into the hills, where Lady Kintore and his daughters had just moved for summer quarters.

The road was excellent, and we had good horses, and managed the distance in an hour and a quarter. This was pretty swift

going, as Marble Hill, the summer residence of the Governor, is 2000 feet above
the sea.   We passed many orchards; every
kind of fruit-tree seems to flourish; the
hay harvest is just beginning, and the
corn begun to be cut.   A very good
crop this year.   The hay is not grass as
with us, but rough corn.   The gardens in
front of the little houses were simply a
blaze of colour, and all the porches and
outhouses covered with flowering creepers.
Quantities of wild roses grew along the
road, and tall Scotch thistles and bracken.
After passing along a very straight street
out of the town, where several congrega-
tions were just coming out of their various
churches, we began to get into the hilly
country.   Little gulleys ran up on each
side of the road, all cultivated by market
gardeners, most of them Chinamen; quantities of cherry-trees and strawberries, and

a profusion of flowers. The gulleys have only good soil at the bottom; the sides being chiefly covered with gum-trees; but by degrees the people make clearings, and in several of these we noticed terraced vineyards covered with vines, trained on little poles. Ash-trees, planes, and elm grow well; but, on account of the dangerous bush fires, the great idea is to make clearings and not to plant trees, especially in the neighbourhood of houses.

Last year they had a very bad fire near Marble Hill, and every man on the place, Lord Kintore at their head, worked energetically to beat it down. They do this by burning a fringe of trees and scrub to meet the fire, but it is desperately hard work, and sometimes they are nearly suffocated by the heat and smoke. Lady Kintore employed herself by carrying cool drinks to the men, who were all much exhausted. We went for a long walk, and they showed us the tracks of the fire and a long series of blackened trunks where it stopped. The view from their villa residence was quite beautiful : range on range of low hills, with gulleys between, were spread out like a map, and in the far distance we caught a glimpse of the ocean. It was extremely cold up there : the weather had been stifling the previous week, ending in a terrific thunderstorm, which made the air deliciously fresh. We gathered bunches of honeysuckle, and a variety of wild flowers, quite different from those at King George's Sound.

· The day passed only too quickly, and after an early dinner at 7 P.M., we drove back under a glorious canopy of stars, to catch the last train for Port Adelaide. The Governor's private saloon carriage, lined with green silk, was put on for us.

We heard, on arriving at the jetty, that the sea had been very rough, and some of the passengers got drenched with the spray going back to the ship, and some were sick. Fortunately it had somewhat quieted down, and we made our little journey in safety. Sunday is very strictly kept in the Colonies, and the cargo could not be unshipped till after twelve o'clock ; so just as we all retired to rest, a tremendous thumping and bumping began overhead, but we were so tired after such a long day that we managed to drop asleep.

The ship did not sail till six in the morning.

A great many passengers have left, so we shall have a little more elbow-room at dinner. We hope to reach Melbourne about two o'clock to-morrow, as we are going along at a good pace, under a brilliant sun and a somewhat rolling blue sea. We have passed a good deal of bare coast scenery, and some rocky islands, and several wild ducks have flown across the bows, evidently making for Kangaroo Island, which we can see in the distance. Lady Kintore had an aviary, with some curious Australian birds called laughing jackasses. They have long yellow beaks, and from time to time they all break into fits of discordant laughter, which has a very weird sound.

P. S. — Arrived safe at Port Philip (Melbourne) on the 22nd November.

LETTER No. 4.

GOVERNMENT HOUSE,
MELBOURNE, 14th December 1892.

IN my last letter I think we had got as far as Adelaide. Now I must tell you a little about Melbourne. We were met at the pier by two of Lord Hopetoun's A.D.C.'s, Lord Northesk and Captain Willoughby ; and right glad we were to leave the ship for good, after saying good-bye to Captain Andrews and some of the officers and passengers. Of course there was a great scramble as soon as the gangway was put across — people struggling on board to see their friends, and those on board equally anxious to get on shore.

We left the maids, with the assistance of a commission agent, to get the luggage through the Custom-House. This agent ran up a pretty bill for his services, and wished to charge us £5 for getting our boxes up to Government House; so I warn all future travellers not to trust to these people, but to see after their luggage themselves, unless they are so wealthy that a few pounds more or less at every port don't signify! In London it only cost 7s. 6d. to hire a van to take my plate chest to the bank in the city, a much further distance, and much heavier boxes.

Government House, where we had a warm welcome, is built rather above the town, and is very like Osborne. I believe it was copied from a picture of the Queen's home in the Isle of Wight. The views over Melbourne from the house and grounds are very pretty, especially at sunset. I have done an oil-painting from my window to give people at home some idea of it all.

The Botanical Gardens join on to those of Government House, and are most beautifully kept. It seems almost impossible to give you an idea of how lovely the flowers and plants and shrubs are here. Geraniums that we take such care of in pots in England grow here almost wild in great bushes and hedges. All kinds of palms and tree ferns also flourish, and some of the tall pine-trees are festooned with crimson roses and yellow banksia roses ; the rhododendrons were also in full bloom, and made masses of colour, the air scented with the perfume of all sorts of delicious plants, and the flower of lime-trees and many flowering shrubs. Beyond the gardens one looks over a lake towards the countless roofs of houses and spires of tall churches and cathedrals, and the puffing smoke from many busy factories and railway trains, hurrying to and fro with goods and passengers. When one considers that forty years ago this vast town was only a little village of wooden houses, the transformation scene is truly wonderful.

Lady Hopetoun drove me all about, and up to the quarter where all the prettiest villas are, surrounded by lovely gardens. She drives her ponies four-in-hand—such a smart little turn out.

I was ,also taken to see the Public Library and picture galleries, and it was like meeting with old friends to see Peter

Graham's *Sunset Glow*, and other works by Davis and Frank Dicksee.

The first thing Australians ask you is, " Well, what do you think of Australia ? " and they are delighted if one honestly admires their country, and especially their own particular colony, although at home we are too much in the habit of lumping them all up together, which is quite wrong. I have several letters from old colonists who came from Buckinghamshire, or had some connection with the Duke's family, giving me a kindly welcome.

Most of the gaieties were over when we reached Melbourne, with the exception of a few garden parties. We went on 29th November to one given by the Bishop of Melbourne and Mrs. Goe. There was a fine old gum-tree in the garden, and as we had not been in an

Australian forest full of them, we admired it very much.

There are fifty different varieties of gums, but people complain very much of the monotony of having only one kind of tree, and no doubt, if one were banished from home for years, one would long for more variety in the vegetation.

A garden party took place at Government House on the 1st December, and we were introduced to a variety of charming people, and much lawn tennis was the order of the day.

Sir Robert and Lady Hamilton, two sons, and a young daughter, arrived that morning from Tasmania on their way to England.

On the 5th we paid a visit to the Zoological Gardens. At the entrance there were some lovely flower beds, and under shady trees a row of gorgeous macaws, cockatoos, and parrots perched on poles attracted our attention—they were all in such beautiful plumage, and so were the eagles and vultures, shrikes, and other birds. It was just feeding-time, and the keeper came round with a pail of raw meat for them ; and afterwards a large truck was brought along with lumps of meat for the lions and tigers, which were also in beautiful condition. Of course it is a very much better climate for them than England. We were shown an ape with a blue and scarlet nose, which is so rare that we were told it was worth £400. It comes from Africa, and is very savage in its captivity. Then we went to see the kangaroos, enclosed in a small grass paddock, and, to our great delight, there were several female kangaroos with their little ones tucked into their pouches. They did look so funny with their little thin paws sticking out, and occasionally a small head appeared and playfully nibbled at its mother's fur, and then retired again into its cosy nest.   It was a very hot day, and we could not linger as long as we should have liked watching the various beasts. Some very handsome Esquimaux dogs seemed to feel the heat a good deal, and so did the brown bears.

There are little white native bears in the woods here, which are occasionally shot ; also a good many snakes.   Five of the latter were killed the other day when we went out rabbit - shooting.   One has to wear long boots as a protection from their poisonous bites.   Very few people die of snake-bites, as even children know how to kill them by a blow with a stick over the middle of the back, which paralyses them ; but it is unsafe to touch a snake's head even if it is cut in two, as it can still bite.

I saw one crawl over a lady's foot; she had incautiously come out to the paddock in house shoes. The snake was trying to get to its hole in an old stump, and one of the shooters ran up and blew it to pieces.

Lady Hopetoun used to flatter herself that the snakes *did not come into the garden* at Government House, up at Mount Macedon; and little Lord Hope was allowed to play about by himself, till one unlucky day when Abraham, the Greek servant, came in triumph with a poisonous adder in a bottle of spirits that had just been captured in the strawberry bed! After that young Hopie was not allowed to go to the orchard without attendance.

The woods are full of all sorts of beautiful little birds. The Australian robin has a wonderfully bright breast, quite orange colour; it is not the least like an English robin. There are some brown birds about the size of a thrush, with long yellow legs and beaks, commonly called "minas." All the notes of the birds sound strange to one at first, till one begins to distinguish them. The laughing jackass is unmistakable. Several tame ones are kept at Government House; they have brownish-gray plumage, and long, sharp beaks, and can be taught to whistle tunes very prettily. The wild parrots have very gay plumage. They do a great deal of damage in the fruit gardens, although they look so pretty about a house, perched on the trees and chattering away to each other.

On Tuesday, 6th December, we moved up to Mount Macedon, a charming cottage, which is the Governor's summer quarters. It is about two hours by rail from Melbourne, and is perched half-way up the

THE EARL OF HOPETOUN.

To face p. 77.

mountain, a good pull for horses from the railway. The Governor, who had preceded us, met us at the station with his four-in-hand brake, and looked extremely happy in his larrikin hat and bush clothes, whip in hand. No more frock coats or uniform for some time to come. The air is very fresh and delicious, and reminds me of Brill Hill, when one drove up there from Wotton on a hot summer's day. It gets rather cold at night, but there are no mosquitoes, and no dust, and no visitors, and we can be out all day long in the forests. We go for long rides, and see beautiful views of the surrounding country. The highest hill is called the Camel's Hump; we rode nearly to the top of it the other day. Sometimes you see a whole side of a hill covered with skeleton trees, as the colonists, to make a clearing, ring the trees, that is, cut a ring right through the bark, thus killing them ; and sometimes forest fires have occurred, and some of these giant skeletons are all charred, and present rather a sad and pitiful spectacle.

All the tram-cars in Melbourne go by electricity ; it makes the streets rather dangerous for carriages and horses. The cabs are buggies with leather hoods, very comfortable in hot weather, and the hansom cabs are all closed round in front with windows and a door, like a small brougham on two wheels.

Buggies are used all over the country ; their wheels are wide apart, and they are very lightly made, and go bounding over obstacles in the bush roads that would certainly cause any other sort of conveyance to come to grief. I must finish up this letter, as, although I seem to have told you almost nothing, it has taken some time to write, owing to many interruptions. We are going to Sydney on the 4th January, so my next letter must be from there.

ROCKS ON MOUNT MACEDON NEAR "CAMEL'S HUMPH."

LETTER No. 5.

HILL VIEW, MOSS VALE,
NEW SOUTH WALES,
21st *January* 1893.

IT is so difficult to remember where I stopped in writing my last letter. I think you have had descriptions of the scenery about Mount Macedon, and the homes of the squatters we went to visit.

We went twice to Melbourne to attend race meetings. The Flemington meeting took place on Monday, 2nd January—a glorious day.

We drove from Government House in

a carriage with four horses and postillions, having left Mount Macedon at eight in the morning. All the stewards, etc., were presented to me on the steps, and we were conducted to the Governor's private box on the Grand Stand, where we had a splendid view of the various events. Besides the flat races, there was a steeple-chase, which included a stone wall and some stiff fences.

Not a single accident occurred, to our great relief, as, on a former occasion, on the 26th December, at Caulfield races, several jockeys came to grief, and one was so much hurt in consequence of his horse and that of his neighbour rolling over him that his life was despaired of. Lady Hopetoun went to see him and his poor mother, who was in great distress. It quite cast a gloom over the rest of the day, but, fortunately, he eventually recovered. The

clerk of the Flemington course took me
all over it, and showed off all the excellent
arrangements for the convenience of the
public, which I think might be copied with
great advantage at home.

The Australians dearly love a holiday,
and no wonder, when they are pretty sure
of a day of cloudless sunshine to enjoy it in.
We also went to see the reporter's room,
and the committee room, and dining-rooms
for various purposes.   The Government
House party were all invited to lunch by
the stewards, and a very excellent one was
provided, especially as we have not been
long enough in the Colonies to despise
cold turkey!   I even heard one fastidious
lady remark that she would rather do
without lunch than eat it.   One can hardly
understand this when one first arrives from
England, where these excellent birds are
a Christmas luxury.

Hilda and I spared a couple of days from our delightful retreat at Mount Macedon to pay a visit to Sir William and Lady Clarke at their charming country place, Rupertswood. We felt the difference of temperature at once on going down from the mountain—especially as, one day, there was a hot wind blowing; but we went out riding all the same, as nothing is so hot as sitting still and thinking about it. We were anxious to see as much as possible of their part of the country. I noticed a good crop of thistles by the side of the roads, and was told that, although there is a tax on thistles in Victoria, Sir William found it better to pay it, as in case of a drought (which the thistles always survive) the sheep would have something to keep them going. We boated in the creek near the house, and played tennis when the sun began to be less fiery, and watched polo practice in the paddock.

On the 22nd we returned to Mount Macedon, the Hopetouns had meanwhile been paying another visit at Point Cook for duck shooting : we were all delighted to meet again and relate our experiences.

Our nearest neighbours, Mr. and Mrs. Ryan, at Macedon, had the most beautiful garden we had yet seen, and one of their daughters, Mrs. Ellice Rowan, is one of the best flower painters in the world.   She was kind enough to show me her collection of wonderful paintings from wild flowers and flowering shrubs, and told me about her adventurous journeys in search of specimens, she having visited wild parts of Queensland and the Islands where no lady had ever been.   She makes friends with the natives, and gets them to procure her rare plants : but she says, their one idea

of helping her is to pull off handfuls of
blossoms, so she can rarely paint from
what they bring her, and has generally to
get them to escort her to the place. She
also paints landscapes marvellously.

The National Art Galleries in Melbourne and Sydney possess several specimens of her flower paintings. I can
describe them as nothing less than gorgeous, and botanically correct as well. In
time, I suppose, names will be found for
the flora of Australia ; at present, the wise
men can only study them, and put them in
Latin classes. This poor lady had just
lost her husband, and her sad pale face
and golden hair, framed in widows' weeds,
haunted me for long afterwards. One of
her sisters is the wife of Admiral Lord
Charles Scott, at whose farewell banquet
at Government House, Melbourne, we had
so recently assisted. We spent Christmas

day very happily in the midst of sunshine and roses; heaps of white flowers and long ferns in the church for decoration.

On *Tuesday, 3rd January*, we started at five in the evening for Hill View, the country place of the Governor of New South Wales (Lord Jersey). It was a very hot afternoon, and the train very crowded with holiday folk; but, fortunately, the directors of the railway had reserved a compartment for us. At about 11 P.M. we reached a junction called Albury, where we changed carriages, and were met by the stationmaster, who presented us with a letter from the directors of the New South Wales Railways, containing passes over their line. It is so funny to be treated as a distinguished foreigner in an English speaking country; in fact, we cannot realise sometimes that we are not at home; everybody is so very kind, and all do their best to make our stay as pleasant as possible.

At Albury we got into a charming sleeping car, where we could undress and turn in with clean sheets and pillows, and sleep soundly all night. I never saw such a huge glorious moon as there was that night, and such a lovely sunrise, which woke us up at an early hour. We were very glad of some cups of hot tea brought by the conductor to our carriage. The lovely sunrise did not last, and we reached Moss Vale Station in a drizzle of rain, and were met by one of the Governor's A.D.C.'s and a covered buggy, in which we drove to Hill View. The house is a sort of rambling bungalow, with deep verandas all round, and stands high. It has been added to in various directions. Lord and Lady Jersey gave us a warm welcome, and so did their young daughters and sons. The country between this and Melbourne is all much the same—forests of gum-trees and occasional clearings, where many "rung" trees toss their skeleton branches over good grass for flocks of sheep. At some of the stations are the beginnings of towns with wide streets, merely laid out, at present green with grass, but no doubt soon to be peopled. Trees have also in many cases been planted on each side of these new streets, and will be ready to shade the population by the time it appears.

On *Friday, 6th January*, Lady Jersey had a small tea party, and we were introduced to some of the ladies who live near, and come up to this country for the summer. You must remember that we are in the middle of summer, and that a north wind means heat and a south wind cold, and that everything is topsy turvy, even the moon doesn't look quite the same

THE EARL OF JERSEY.   *To face p. 89.*

as at home. Jackasses sit in the trees and laugh loudly at their own jokes (they are really birds, and prey upon smaller ones, which they spear with their sharp beaks).

On *Saturday, 7th*, I attended a cricket match with Lady Jersey ; his Excellency and staff were playing in it. The attendance of spectators was not large, as the ladies care more for lawn tennis.

On *Sunday* we all walked to church in a broiling sun, about a mile off, and a good many more people were presented to me after service. One lady told Lady Jersey that she was so glad to have seen a real live duchess. This made me laugh, as I don't feel the least duchessy, and now they all call me the " real live one." They tell me I am the first duchess who has ever come to the Colonies.

On *Monday, 8th*, we all started for Sydney at nine o'clock, lunched at Government House, and sketched in the garden, which slopes down to the harbour. It is a lovely view ; the house is a castellated one, and was built in 1830. The reception rooms are now not nearly large enough, as the guests to be entertained are far more numerous, and it entails having a greater number of banquets and balls. In the principal drawing-room many full-length portraits of George III. and Queen Charlotte in their youth, very like those on the staircase at Wotton. There is a pleasing portrait of the Queen, and a very poor one of the Princess of Wales in the drawing-room, also various portraits and busts of different governors.

The climate at Sydney is very enervating ; and people feel the heat there much in the summer, and all who can, fly to the mountains. We were only a few hours in the town, did some necessary shopping, and started again at 5 P.M.

for the Blue Mountains—a trip we had arranged to take with the Jerseys and their family. Our first stage was the hotel at Mount Victoria, and a beautiful journey it was, the railway gradually ascending till we reached a ridge of mountains, and on each side were fine views over forests into the valleys. We passed the Nepean river with its wooded banks, before entering the first mountain gorge, where we thought we should have been almost suffocated in a tunnel, the heat of the steam was so tremendous. We all rushed to the windows on emerging to see if the train was on fire. It was a tiring day, and we were delighted when we reached our destination. The garden of the hotel was all streaming with flags of all colours in honour of the Governor. Next morning a photographer arrived, and asked to take a group on the steps ;

after which we all mounted into various coaches, with four horses each, and drove thirty - seven miles through fine bush scenery, over mountains to the Jenolan Caves, stopping first to see some sheep-shearing in a shed at the house of a selector ; and again, in the middle of the day, at a Rest-house, where we lunched on turkeys as usual, and puddings and stewed fruit, the mistress of the house having a hard time of it cooking and waiting on such a large party. It was very difficult to get everybody seated in the small room, and in the parlour some of the party had to sit on the floor. It was a relief, however, to get out of the glare into a dark, if not a cool room.

The Wilsons were most hospitable, and did their best to make us comfortable. They said it was very difficult to get provisions in such an out of the way part, and that we must excuse the roughness of the repast. It really was beautifully cooked, and most excellent for hungry travellers. The sheep we saw sheared were the most sensible animals I have ever met, for they seemed to know perfectly what was going to be done, and sat quite still like a dog begging, while their wool was removed very rapidly with the shears. One other halt we made at the garden gate of a squatter named Young, whose family presented the Governor and Lady Jersey with various floral trophies.

THE HOPETOUNE'S COACH.
(*From a Photograph by her Ladyship.*)

THE FITZROY FALLS.

LETTER No. 6

HILL VIEW, MOSS VALE,
NEW SOUTH WALES,
23rd January 1893.

Now I must tell you about our arrival at the
Jenolan Caves after the long thirty-seven
mile drive in a blazing sun.   It got cooler
towards evening, and, as the shadows
began to lengthen, and the valleys of the
Blue Mountains got bluer and bluer, we
at length rounded the last steep corner,
and halted on the verge of a precipice

protected by a stout fence, where a few
other coaches and buggies were drawn up.
It seemed difficult to realise that we were
to disembark here, as there was no sign
of human habitation, a natural rampart of
rocks appearing to bar our further pro-
gress. However, in a few minutes we
were marching by a footpath down a
gorge, and entering the huge black mouth
of a cavern. On the giant rocks over-
hanging the streams were perched about
ninety visitors, who welcomed the Governor
and his party with hearty cheers, and the
music of "God save the Queen" from a
brass band, the cheers echoing loudly from
the surrounding rocks, which towered above
us till they formed a complete wall across
the gorge. Half - way up there was a
beautiful natural archway through which
the setting sun streamed brilliantly, and
we realised for the first time what cheering

to the echo meant. We entered the cavern, which soon began to widen, and after walking along the bed of the stream, over rough stones, and crossing it twice on small planks, we eventually emerged into sunshine again, and found ourselves in a narrow valley and close to the Cave House. It was kept by a Mr. Wilson and his wife, who came to welcome us, and informed the Governor that they took it as a happy omen that we should have fixed on their silver wedding-day to arrive at the caves. This man is also guide, and a perfect enthusiast. He began his career before the road we travelled by was made, the only other being for pack horses and riders, who usually slept in the caves in the blankets they brought with them.

A very substantial repast of sucking pig and roast mutton awaited us, after a pre-

liminary cup of tea and a rest in the
veranda. After dinner we all started for
the largest cave, called the " Devil's Coach-
House," which was most beautifully illuminated in our honour with different coloured
fires, till every part of the marvellous formation of the roof stood out, its beauties fully
revealed. This cave is 300 feet high,
and nothing we saw afterwards could
come up to the beauty of this nocturnal
illumination. It was rather difficult to
clamber about and keep your footing in
the semi-darkness.

Next morning (*Wednesday, January*
11) we breakfasted at nine o'clock, and
started for some of the other caves,
armed with candles, and explored the
Lucinda, the Architect's Studio, the Mys-
tery, Katie's Bower, Lady Carrington's
Heaven and Hell—a sort of vestibule leading to some of the smaller ones, in which

there was a stalactite exactly like a statue of a mother and child, called the Madonna. We were also shown a statuette of St. Patrick in one of the smaller caves. In some of the passages there were wonderful formations like blankets or shawls, with a border draping from the roof; others formed pillars. Our guide had a lantern with magnesium light, which he constantly cast into dark corners, and through gaping chasms, bringing all sorts of wonderful transparent formations to light.

In the afternoon most of the party started again for the Jersey Cave and underground river, to which you descend on a wire rope ladder. In spite of the fascinations of this expedition, I decided to remain above ground, and spent the afternoon doing a sketch of the Carlotta Arch, as I wished to have some remem-

CARLOTTA ARCH, JENOLAN CAVES.

To face p. 93.

brance to take away with me of this delightful and mysterious place.

On *Thursday, 12th*, we left the Cave House, after promising to send our photos to the Wilsons. Walking in a long procession to the starting-place, laden with bags and bundles of every description, we commenced our return journey, doing fifty miles that day to Katoomba, making a halt at the Rest House for lunch, and again for tea at Mount Victoria. We noticed some birds, called gung-gungs, rather like gray pigeons, but, as a rule, the great forests we drove through were very silent and devoid of bird life ; and from the coach, of course, we did not hear the hum of numerous insects and the chirp of grasshoppers.

In olden days the Kelly gang and other bushrangers played the police many a trick by their superior knowledge of

the Jenolan Caves and their various wind-
ings, and we heard stories of their being
tracked to the mouth of one or other of
them, and the police sitting down quietly
to wait for them, while all the time they
had made off quite safely and happily
across the mountains by some other outlet.
At Katoomba Hilda and I descended
at the Carrington Hotel, while the
Governor and his family drove to Lillian-
fields, to stay with the Chief-Justice Sir
Frederick Darley. After roughing it at
smaller inns, this hotel seemed wonderfully comfortable and even magnificent;
we thoroughly enjoyed our stay there.
The view from our veranda was very
extensive; on all sides ranges and ranges
of mountains, as far as the eye could
reach. Of course the garden was full of
roses, gladioli, pansies, etc., and the
dinner table covered with flowers. All

THE THREE SISTERS   BLUE MOUNTAINS.

To face p. 191.

the people staying there were very anxious to see us, watching for us on the steps every time we went out.

Hilda and I were thoroughly done up after this fifty mile drive in the great heat, and rather depressed at parting from our fellow-travellers, and setting up for ourselves at the hotel; so I proposed we should indulge in the extravagance of a pint of Heidsieck Très-sec., which was highly successful in restoring our exhausted frames.

On *Friday, 13th*, the Darleys asked us to join their party, and took us to see the Wentworth Falls, where, in spite of the heat and flies (which are perfect torments to artists), I made a hasty sketch of one of the red and yellow sandstone cliffs, and later in the day managed to get another done of some famous red rocks called the Three Sisters. The difficulty was to find a suitable spot, and after a severe struggle I contrived to establish myself on the edge of a precipice, on some very dry and slippery rocks, where there was only the ghost of a footpath ; I had to assure Sir Frederick Darley that I would do my level best not to roll after the easel, or try to catch it if it were suddenly blown down the ravine.

On *Saturday, 14th*, we made a grand picnic expedition with the whole united party to a place called Govett's Leap. Oh, such a beautiful, wonderful place ! An amphitheatre of cliffs, occasionally intersected with dashing waterfalls. The trees at the foot of these cliffs looked like little cabbages, and were so close and thick, and covered with creepers, that we could only see their tops. The skeleton of a man was found somewhere down there in the thick bush ; he must have strayed from his friends, and got lost and bewildered in the endless scrub and forest.

We made a little fire very carefully, so as not to set fire to the trees, in the bush, and cooked some potatoes; and after a careful examination of the ground to see there were no snakes, we all sat down and had an excellent repast, several neighbours having joined the party, and brought contributions to the picnic. Two of them told me they had a Singalese cook, who had rushed after them at the last moment with a card-box containing cheese straws, as she was most anxious Lady Jersey should partake of her artistic savoury; and they promised to tell the black girl how much we appreciated her skill.

Before returning home, after scrambling down to the falls, and leaning over the precipice, and throwing stones to see if we could hear them fall, they said we must have some "billy tea," which is what everybody makes out here. A billy is a tin can which is filled with water and put on the fire. The tea is thrown into it as soon as the water begins to boil. The driver meanwhile recited some of his own poetry all about Govett's Leap, and also a funny piece called the " Laughing Jackass," in praise of those birds I told you about. He called them the "squatters' clocks," and said they were so convenient as they did not require winding up ; every verse ended with a chorus of " Hee, hee, hee !"

On the way home we were caught in a tremendous thunderstorm, and got well soaked—hailstones like peas (the papers next morning said pigeons' eggs!) and sheets of rain. It rains like a waterspout here when it once begins. Some of the ladies were so frightened that they took refuge in a house, but most of us drove on and braved the elements. Fortunately we had taken some warm coats, as this climate is not to be trusted, and the changes come on so suddenly.

We heard many stories of bushranging times. An uncle of young Darley (who drove me in his pony cart) had an exciting experience. He returned from some expedition, driving his buggy, with a friend following on horseback, to find his station stuck up. They both thought something was wrong when they saw all the station hands sitting in a row on the rail; however, he drove up to the door of his house, and sure enough he was met on the step by a bushranger armed with a revolver in each hand, who yelled to him to " Bail up," that is, throw up your arms and surrender. Of course, in face of two revolvers, he had no other course but to say, "All right," and he got down from the buggy and proceeded to unfasten the leader, his favourite mare, and send her flying into the bush with a cut of his whip, determined *she* should not fall a prey to the bushranger, who was all the time explaining that he had slain a man in a scuffle with the police, and must have a fast horse to help him to escape across the boundary. The squatter slowly proceeded to the stables, where his unwelcome guest wished to choose a saddle, trying all the time to get an opportunity of slinking behind the man and pouncing on him, but he was too sharp, and quickly ordered the squatter to march in front of him.

On returning to the house the bushranger asked, "Have you any arms in the buggy?" "Yes, two revolvers." "Get them out," said the man. "Get them out for yourself, they are just under the seat," answered the squatter in a tone of authority, and on the impulse of the moment his enemy stretched over to look under the seat. This was the opportunity he had been longing for, and being a big, powerful man, he threw himself with his whole weight on the bushranger, and of course the station hands all came to his assistance, and his friend also who had been lurking behind in hopes of being able to help. In the scuffle the revolver went off, tearing the squatter's thumb.

The man was bound hand and foot, and some one galloped off for the police, who arrived very speedily. He was soon after hung, and he said it was all his own folly, as he might have known it was no good trying to " stick up " Sylvester Brown's station.

Strange to say, we saw this enormous squatter on the *Arcadia ;* he embarked at Adelaide, and is the brother of the man who writes under the name of Rolf Boldrewood and is the author of *Robbery Under Arms*, and other splendid stories.

One other tale I must tell you about him. He has explored in some of the wildest parts of Queensland, and discovered a strong, handsome tribe of blacks, with whose chief he made friends; and the natives respected his immense size and strength, as hitherto they had never seen a man to equal their own chief. He noticed that there seemed very few children in the tribe, and after he had been with them some time and gained their confidence, they told him that the fact was they ate any superfluous children they did not want to grow up!

Lady Darley told us of an adventure she quite well remembered which befell her and two of her brothers when they were

from four to six years old. They lived
with their parents on Boldrewood Station,
in Victoria, and one day their elders left
them in charge of the servants, who, however, went off themselves to some merry-
making. This unfortunate moment was
the time chosen by a tribe of blacks to
make a descent on the station. The
children were very frightened, but the
eldest boy's first idea was to seize a gun
to defend them all. This was most dangerous, as they tried to drag it to some
hiding-place, but failing in their efforts,
they abandoned the idea, and boldly faced
the black chief and his party, who made
them understand that they had come for
food, and that clothing would also be
acceptable. The children managed to
satisfy their demands, as they knew where
the meat and flour were kept, and trotted
backwards and forwards till they could

find no more, and then proceeded to bestow some of their own clothes on the un-welcome visitors, who eventually professed themselves satisfied, and took their departure.

Lady Darley says she well remembers what a state her mother was in when she returned and found what had happened, as the children had run a great risk of being killed or carried off. I must now wind up this lengthy letter, and reserve our proceedings in Sydney for another mail.

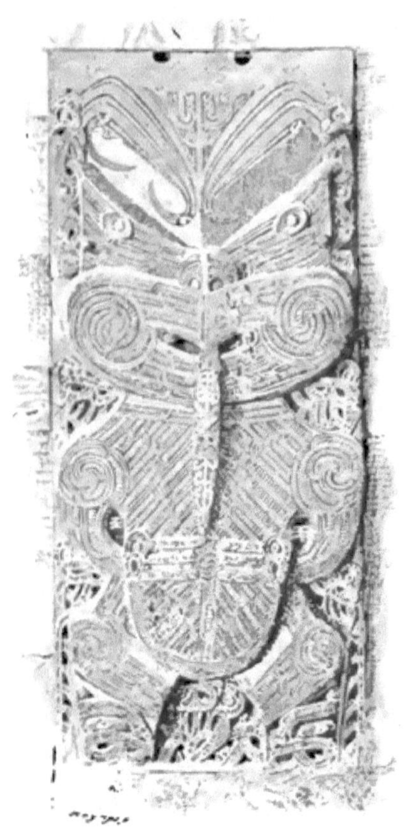

MAORI CARVING.

LETTER No. 7.

GOVERNMENT YACHT "HINEMOA,"
MILFORD SOUND, SOUTH ISLAND,
NEW ZEALAND, 10*th February* 1893.

ON *Monday, 16th January*, we reluctantly bade adieu to the Blue Mountains, and started for Sydney in the Governor's luxurious saloon carriage.

At Katoomba railway station a crowd of school children, marshalled by their teachers, were waiting to see us. Lady Jersey and I went to talk to them. I told them they were very lucky children to live in such a beautiful climate, and asked how they would like all the snow and frost that was going on in England. Such rows of bright, sunburnt faces! I do think people have more habitually cheerful expressions out here, as they are not always contending with the elements, and keeping their eyes half-shut to prevent themselves being blinded by wind and snow and rain. They all cheered lustily as we steamed off.

That evening the whole party went to the circus, and saw some wonderful acrobats and riding. One girl rode through flaming hoops, lying on a bare-backed white horse, all her dark hair flowing over its side.

Another did juggling tricks of throwing up knives and catching them, standing on horseback all the time ; she also afterwards walked on a wire hung about fifteen feet from the ground. She had some white doves on her shoulder ; they were very tame, and fluttered round her head, not a bit dismayed by the flaring gas jets. She was a pretty, fair girl, and looked as if she would be happier at home with needles and thread than doing all these wonderful things. Some little girls also danced on the wires. There was one strong man, who carried two or three other athletes as if he enjoyed it. They had an exhibition of fighting men with shields and spears, and also contests with daggers. The shields made a great deal of clattering, and it all looked very dangerous. Afterwards some Japanese conjurers performed, and one little boy did some contortionist feats which were much more curious than pretty. The most amusing thing was when the clown's pig came into the circus and performed a walk over, jumping a succession of hurdles amidst the applause of the audience; the pig and the clown made a capital couple.

Wednesday, 18th January.—After this frivolity we had a day at the Museum, where we were met and shown over it by Dr. Ramsay, who has special charge of the stuffed birds and eggs, and is an excellent ornithologist. Dr. Cox, Crown Trustee and Conchologist, showed us all the shells and curious native arms and masks. There were some huge food bowls which a whole tribe eat out of; occasionally portions of human beings were served up in them. Some of the war canoes were very beautifully adorned with cowrie shells, and the paddles carved.

The masks used for the " devil dances "
were very hideous and extremely heavy,
adorned with bunches of cockatoo feathers
at the top, and cut out of solid wood,
painted red, blue, white, and brown, and
fixed on a short pole or stick.

We were given a couple of king birds-
of-paradise, their plumage orange and
gold-coloured, and two long feathers in
the tail with green eyes at the end.
These birds are very rare. I also got
a small box with some brilliant green
beetles, and Hilda had a boomerang,
which is a piece of flat wood like a curved
paper knife ; the Australian blacks throw
it an immense distance with deadly effect.
They also gave me a pair of armlets made
of bone ; they are sometimes worn hanging
from a chain round the neck ; and next
day Dr. Cox sent me a stuffed platypus.
This is a most extraordinary animal, a sort

of cross between a duck and a beaver; it has a duck's bill and webbed feet, and its skin is more like a mole or an otter with a white breast, so soft and furry. He also sent us a stick insect. It is exactly like a little branch of a tree, and hangs by its claws quite motionless for hours; if one touches it, two little green wings, which look just like leaves, begin to sprout. We were so afraid it would escape, so we put it in a waste paper basket topsy turvy, and decided to give it some chloroform. but, strange to say, this had no effect; it only went to sleep for a little while; so we tried it with a drop of laudanum. and that had no effect; but when we offered it a drop of water it responded at once, and I saw its mouth open, and a funny little red tongue lapped up the drops. However the drugs must have disagreed with it, for it died next day, and, unfortunately.

was swept up by the housemaid, who, no doubt, thought it was only a stupid little piece of dead wood and not a wonderful stick insect at all.

At three o'clock we went to hear the organ recital in the Town Hall. This organ is the largest in the world, and was skilfully played by Mons. Auguste Wiegand, the city organist. He gave us a concerto in B flat by Handel, and a song by Blumenthal, preludum and fugue in G major by Bach, toccata in A flat (St. Cecilia Collection) by Adolph Hesse, Le Ruisseau by Gounod, a march by Cherubini, etc., etc. It really was most refreshing to hear some good music again; and if we had had time we would have descended from our state gallery, where we sat with the Mayor of Sydney and his wife, and asked the organist to play some of our favourite pieces.

The Town Hall is in most beautiful proportion, and the great white organ makes a splendid finish to it at one end. We returned to Moss Vale at five o'clock.

On *Thursday*, 10*th*, we all started in buggies for the picnic races at Bong Bong, about seven miles from Hill View. After driving to within a mile of the race-course, we left the high road and proceeded along a bush track through paddocks, bowling along over the grass, with an occasional bump into a rut or over a stump.

The racing was most amusing, and everybody picnicked in booths and tents erected under the green trees at the back of the stand, which consisted of an open shed, where many pretty ladies in smart hats and summer dresses were congregated, taking the deepest interest in each event, as all the horses belonged to their various brothers, fathers, and cousins, and were generally ridden by the owners.

It was a gay scene and quite unlike anything we had ever seen before. The prizes were chiefly jewelry, which were afterwards given to the ladies by the winners. The excitement rose to fever pitch when one race ended in a dead heat between two horses, called Nightlight and Jester. The weather was perfect, and the meeting lasted two days; but having had such a hard week we were glad of a rest next day, so did not accompany Lord Jersey and his daughters.

We had several hospitable invitations to visit different stations in the Colony, but, alas! there was not time to accept them.

Sydney is by far the most beautifully situated town we have seen, and the sites for country houses and villas round the harbour are most lovely. Unfortunately the sea was rough, so our only sight of the Heads was from the shore. Lady Jersey took us a beautiful drive to some heights above the town, whence we had a distant view of Botany Bay, and the harbour was spread out like a map. We contented ourselves with a short cruise up the Paramatta River in the Government steam-launch.

On *Tuesday*, 24*th*, we started on our return journey to Melbourne from Hill View. We were sorry to end our visit to New South Wales, although, considering the short time we were there, I think we managed to see as much as possible.

We left by the evening train, arrived about twelve o'clock next morning, and were heartily welcomed home at Government House by the Hopetouns, who were in the midst of packing up for their New

Zealand trip. We had a most cheerful evening, and various songs from the A.D.C.'s after dinner.

On *Thursday*, 26*th*, we saw the Hopetouns on board the *Warrimoo*, shivering over the thoughts of the rough passage they were in for, as the sea always is rough between these coasts, because you get the whole force of the Southern Ocean when off New Zealand.

We intended to embark for the Bluff on Friday, but on returning to Government House with Captain Forbes and Mr. Wallington, who were left behind to assist in carrying on the government, we heard that the steamship company had changed our ship and the day of starting, so, instead of getting off in the *Rotohama* on Friday, we were shunted on to the *Te Anau*, a smaller and slower boat, which only left Melbourne on Saturday.

At one o'clock we were on board, and although we were supposed to make a very good passage, and had a capital state cabin, with lots of room and gilt carved wood cherubs' heads at all the corners, still we were not happy.

The little ship plunged about in the choppy sea; it was bitterly cold on deck, and besides, the decks were encumbered with carcases of dead sheep and a fruit cargo packed in wooden boxes, that towered like a wall and prevented any walking about. Our state cabin was situated exactly over the screw, and, being a deck one, the noisy conversation of the other passengers was very audible. Oh, dear me! what would not one have given to get that horrid screw to stop for half-an-hour? it felt at last as if a gimlet was being screwed into one's backbone; and our berths were as hard as doors, and we were as stiff as pokers, and too ill even to make jokes. Thankful were we to reach Bluff Harbour, and come to anchor at six in the morning on Thursday, 2nd February, having had five days on the briny ocean—almost as long as it takes to go to America from Liverpool.

Owing to our change of boat, and being in consequence a day late, we missed the trip to Stewart Island with Lord and Lady Glasgow, who judged rightly that after our long voyage we would be the better of some hours' rest at the hotel before starting afresh.

We walked up the wide street of the little town, and came to a provision shop, where strange shells, spears, models of canoes, and other curiosities were on view. I bought a huge turtle shell, and Hilda got a small one; they are to come home in a meat ship next month.

Curiously enough, the landlord of the hotel was deeply interested in our arrival, as he came from Peeblesshire, and had been in service in Sir Adam Hay's family. I climbed the hill behind the town, and re-joiced in the delicious flower-scented air and bright sunshine.

A young butcher boy passed on a capital horse, so I asked him if there were any ponies with a lady's saddle for hire. He said his master's daughter had one; it was the only one in the place, but he was sure he would be delighted to lend it to me. I proceeded to inter-view the daughter of the butcher, but, alas! the saddle had just had all the stuffing taken out, and was hanging on the garden fence in a most dilapi-dated condition; so, with many civil speeches, I reluctantly gave up the idea of reaching the top of the hill, and only

THE EARL OF GLASGOW.   *To face p.* 123.

went as far as my own legs would carry me.

It is perfectly extraordinary how friendly every one is in the Colonies, and how they go out of their way to oblige you if they possibly can. About five o'clock the Glasgows returned, and we went on board the *Hinemoa*, and were introduced to everybody. The party, besides Lord and Lady Glasgow, consists of two daughters, one son, a cousin, the military secretary, Colonel Pat. Boyle, Captain Clayton, A.D.C., and Mr. G——, the tutor; and in addition to Hilda and me as visitors, there were Lady Kintore and two daughters.

After dinner we weighed anchor, and had a calm passage to Otago Retreat, Preservation Inlet. We were stopped by a sand-bar at the mouth of the Inlet, but got in another way, and now began our voyage through the "Western Sounds" of New Zealand. They are so wonderful and beautiful that it seems quite impossible to give you any idea of them on paper. We saw traces of the mining population along the shore, as gold has lately been found here. Landed some stores for the lighthouse people, steamed out to sea again, and just before lunch we anchored at Dusky Sound, and proceeded to Captain Cook's anchorage in Pickersgill Harbour, where I sketched the mountains in a frantic hurry for an hour, while some of the party landed to take photographs and get bitten by the sandflies which infest these parts of the shore. The worst of these flies is that they follow you on board, and continue their feast regardless of execrations and the numbers of the slain. However, we may be thankful there are no mosquitoes.

That night we anchored in Wet Jacket Arm, off Dusky Sound, passing the most marvellous formation of mountains, towering straight above us in most fantastic shapes, covered nearly to the top with beautiful bush, fir, pines, and birch, and all sorts of beautiful tree ferns and creepers, and brilliant yellow and green moss.

On *Saturday, 4th February*, got up at seven, and accompanied the bathers, who had been busy for two days making swimming dresses for themselves. We rowed to the head of the creek, I taking my sketching things and managing to do a sketch, in spite of the vigorous onslaught of our insect foes, who literally bit my hands till they bled. Saw some colonial robins, so tame they almost lighted on one's head ; also some oyster birds, or " red bills," with black bodies and red legs and beaks.

We were ravenous for breakfast, after which repast we steamed up Anchor Passage to Breaksea Sound, and up Vancouver Arm, where we landed in the boats and explored in the bush to our great delight. I spied two native crows, large gray birds, with red patches on each side of their heads.

It is very exciting landing in unknown creeks, which no foot of man has ever trod before, not knowing if the boat won't get aground. We then steamed up Broughton Arm, and I did a large sketch of some wonderful peaks and a gorge. We saw some cow fish gamboling in the water; they are enormous creatures, running to fourteen feet long, and rather like porpoises. They jumped right out of the water in their astonishment when the yacht passed.

In the afternoon we put out to sea

and had two hours of pitching and tossing, till at last we anchored for the night in Dagg's Sound.

Captain Fairchild told a number of amusing Maori stories at dinner, especially about all the tricks that went on at the time of the war. When the Maories were in want of bullets they used to show a dummy in the bush ; of course it was immediately fired at. A man with a string in the background pulled it down. "Oh," thought our fellows, "we've done for him." Up came the dummy again, cautiously ; bang, bang, bang went the rifles of the British troops ; down fell dummy ; and this went on till some worse marksman than usual cut the dummy's rope, and no Maori would go up the tree to splice it, as it was certain death to do so. The bullets were all taken out of a little earth bank they had made behind the tree where the dummy appeared. This dodge was not discovered for a long time.

On *Sunday, 5th Feb.*, Lord Glasgow read morning service in the saloon ; very heavy showers. We landed to inspect a waterfall, and got drenched. After lunch put out to sea. Hilda and I sat on deck holding on tight, as the *Hinemoa* is given to rolling. The entrance to Smith Sound was gained, the mountains looking very mysterious, veiled in clouds and mist,— the great rocks covered with sea-birds and yellow sea-weed at the entrance. We anchored that night in Hall's Arm, Smith Sound.

On *Monday, 6th February*, several boat-loads landed to explore the creeks. The " larrikins," as we called the young and giddy portion of this crew, headed by Mr. G—— with a small axe, found the bush so impenetrable that, as the only means of getting back to the shore, they kilted their petticoats and waded down a creek, clearing the branches as they went.

I embarked with the mate in the ship's gig, which was sent to fetch them, and never shall I forget the absurd scene when they all emerged wet and dripping from under the branches of bush scrub that met overhead. We had forced the boat up the narrow channel as far as it would go, and came upon several birds, a native crow, and a male and female fantail—lovely little birds like slender canaries, only brown, with white tails, which they constantly open and shut like a fan.

The girls all bathed again, not content with one wetting. They swim beautifully, and the savage rocks echo back shouts of laughter.

We are a subject of great curiosity to all the wild birds, who seem quite tame, and not the least aware what dangerous creatures we are. Beautiful waterfalls stream down the mountains in all directions.

At 2.30 we weighed anchor and steamed into Bradshaw Sound, where we caught sight of a pair of wild swans and four young cygnets. The engines were stopped, and the captain was off and after them in the twinkling of an eye ; he returned shortly with a very pleased smile on his weather-beaten face and a live cygnet under each arm. The bathers also contributed to the menagerie by catching some penguins. They are the most ridiculous birds, with little hard fins for wings, and webbed feet and long sharp bills, green backs, and yellow or white breasts. They hop and swim, but can't fly, and are most cheeky and impertinent. Their antics on deck amused the whole party. We anchored in Gair Arm, Bradshaw Sound.

On *Tuesday, 7th February*, started at 9 A.M., in pouring rain, down Bradshaw and Thompson Sounds, reached Caswell Sound at one o'clock after two hours tossing at sea. Weather cleared up in the evening, and I sketched from a boat with Hilda and Mr. G——. We were drifting slowly down the sound, quite unconscious, occupied with our painting, when suddenly we heard the steam-whistle of the yacht warning us it was time to turn, so we had a hard row back against the tide, and lucky we found it out in time, or they would have had to weigh anchor and come after us.

On *Wednesday, 8th February*, left Caswell Sound at 5 A.M., reached Bligh Sound at 8.30. Splendid weather ; landed in boat at Bounty Haven, found shells,

pampas grass, and a white flowery shrub
with blossom like a large daisy with
brown heart; also a tiny white orchid
with delicious smell.   Brought a lot of
green branches on board for the cow, and
did two sketches after lunch, had two
hours of a beautiful pitchy torquoise sea,
and sketched Mount Pembroke with its
snowy peak.   Anchored at mouth of
Milford Sound for fishing and scrambling
purposes.   Landed and found an old bush
track and dilapidated miner's hut; collected
various ferns, and with help of axe cut
several sticks and supple Jack canes, and
found some oval white marble stones on
the shore for painting on.   Caught some
penguins.

The scenery on entering Milford Sound
baffles description, especially as we saw
it first in a glorious sunset, with snow-
capped peaks in the distance illuminated with

MITRE PEAK, MILFORD SOUND, NEW ZEALAND.

To face p. 114.

pink and golden lights intensified by deep blue shadows — great walls of granite coming on each side straight down into the sea. At length we turned the last corner, and were anchored in full view of Mitre Peak and Mount Pembroke.

Thursday, 9th February.—With much reluctance I bundled out of bed at 5 A.M. in order to see and sketch the sunrise, which was very lovely. That morning Miss H—— started with Mr. Miller, Eddie, and Mr. G——, to walk to the Sutherland Falls; but, before they reached Lake Ada, poor B—— sprained her ankle. Not thinking it was serious, she walked a little way to the boat which took them to the head of the lake; by this time her foot was much swollen and very painful, and it was decided that she and her cousin would have to remain for the night at the roadmaker's hut. There they met with great hospitality, and were regaled on a supper of eels and billy tea, and in spite of the sandflies and other insect pests, seem to have had a festive time, although they missed the grand sight of the Sutherland Falls.

At 12.30 started in a boat with Lord and Lady Glasgow, Lady Kintore and daughters, Captain Boyle, and Captain Clayton, up Arthur River. Here we landed at the former penal settlement, where the convicts' old huts still remain. Walked for two miles to Lake Ada through a superb mountain gorge, through which the Arthur River had to fight its way amongst giant boulders, making a dull sound of waterfall in the depths beneath. We saw a hawk floating in the blue sky, and a great chattering of small birds in the bush, as if they were passing a warning note round to their friends. I saw some lovely little green tits going about in pairs ; they had gray breasts and sort of bright sea-green eye-brows and no tails—most fascinating little birds.

It was very rough rowing back to the hotel at the head of the sound, kept by a man called Sutherland, who lately married a handsome widow. There we had tea, and had to wait for the return of the *Hinemoa*. Captain Fairchild had gone to land some stores and mail bags at Martin's Bay and Big Bay. The sea was rough, and some of those who remained on board suffered for it. We met an artist at the hotel named Perret, who had done some rather pretty little oil pictures. Lord Glasgow and Lady Kintore bought several of them. The *Hinemoa* did not return till after sunset, and we had to walk through a bush path, beset with snares for the unwary, to reach the boats. I christened a grand mountain peak " Mount Chandos," and they are going to send the name up for the Government maps. There was a beautiful sunset that evening, but sunsets only last a very few moments in this country, so it is very difficult to get the colouring in a sketch.

Friday, 10*th February*, was rather cloudy and cold, with occasional heavy rain.

Hilda and I, accompanied by various members of the party, landed near the Bowen Falls, and had a most exhausting climb up a precipitous bush path to see the falls from the top. In some places steps were cut in the rocks, or made by roots of trees, and occasionally ropes were stretched at the most dangerous places for us to swing ourselves up by ; it was like climbing the wall of a house. Those who eventually reached the over-hanging rocks, where the water was dashing down, said it was a very fine sight, but, alas! I was not of the number. We were thoroughly soaked before we got back to the yacht, and started that night for Westport.

All *Saturday, Feb.* 11*th*, we were at sea, stopped occasionally to land stores, and had a glorious peep of Mount Cook, Mount Tasman, and a range of snowy peaks. They rose out of the clouds, as there was a good deal of mist along the shore, so we were most lucky to get a sight of them. We had been going for some miles along the coast in perfect despair at the fog, when at length one peak appeared like a large white star; you would hardly believe it was a mountain, and it looked quite up in the heavens. The sea was a wonderful green colour, and gradually the clouds parted like a curtain, and there was the marvellous range exposed to view against a bright blue sky. All those who had retired to their cabins, victims of the deceitful ocean, were routed out to see the wonderful sight.

Hilda and I managed to remain on deck, and had our deck chairs lashed to the mast. Towards evening it calmed down, and after we all got to bed we did not mind what happened.

Early on Saturday morning we anchored in Westport Harbour. It was delightful to get on shore, and the air was delicious— a lovely day, quite hot. We walked to St. John's Church, and were met half-way by a procession of volunteer sailors, who came to do honour to the Governor, but were rather too late to catch him on the *Hinemoa*, as we were not expected to arrive till Monday.

We walked along the river's bank by a bush path admiring the tree ferns and creepers, and hoping for fine weather to continue.

Our further doings at Westport I must reserve for another mail.

BREAKSEA SOUND.

LETTER No. 8.

Tavistock Hotel,
Waipukurau, Hawkes Bay,
North Island, New Zealand.
9th March 1893.

I THINK my last letter ended on our safe arrival in Westport Harbour on Sunday the 19th February. Enclosed are some newspaper cuttings, which may interest you, and will save me a lot of extra writing. The earthquake described took place that morning, and although we were all up and dressed, and strolling about on the pier at eight o'clock, waiting for breakfast, none of us were aware of the shock.   As there was to be an earthquake we felt rather defrauded not to have noticed it.

The sun shone brightly, and all looked so calm and peaceful after the stormy sea.

I walked to church with the Governor and some of the party.   The volunteers were sent to meet us, and Lord Glasgow inspected them, and spoke to their officer. They were all dressed as sailors, although they rarely, if ever, go to sea.

On *Monday*, 13*th*, it poured torrents of rain, so our expedition had to be postponed. The railway manager, Mr. Peterkin, who is an Aylesbury man, and worked under the Duke on the London and North-Western in former days, brought his daughter to present me with some flowers. He had one of the goods-sheds converted into a temporary drawing-room, and we were very glad to make use of it, and paint, read, and work there, instead of being cooped up on board the yacht. Later in the day some of the party went by train to see the harbour works.

The next day (*Tuesday, 14th February*) we made a grand expedition to Denniston coal mines, organised by Mr. Miller, who is one of the directors, and also Speaker of the Upper House.

All went by train as far as Waimangaroa, where we got out to inspect a gold mine. The fortunate miner it belongs to makes from £20 to £30 a week. Hilda and Lady Augusta Boyle and her brother descended into the mine. You go down a long slanting passage, in a crouching position, getting your clothes covered with wet yellow mud. The earth is brought out in a little truck and poured with water into a long wooden trough, with a sort of wooden ladder in it to catch the grains of gold. The gravel and mud are all carried into the river, but the gold, being so heavy, sinks to the bottom. We were presented with some small bits of gold, and I got a little nugget.

The miner was delighted at the ladies going down his mine, as he said the ladies of Westport would not do it : they were frightened, and did not like getting wet.

Then we all scrambled back into our special train, and went on a short distance to the foot of the mountain, to see the coal trucks coming spinning down from the top. As the mountain is 2000 feet high, you may imagine the pace is terrific. The loaded truck draws the empty one up by an arrangement of twisted wire ropes.

This plan is perfectly successful, but the engineers were some time finding it out, and used to have rather serious accidents with the trucks, as formerly before the road was made through the bush, all the women and children went up that way. Even now the trucks sometimes get off the lines and collide with each other. We remounted our train, and steamed back to Waimangaroa Station, where a crowd was collected to see the cavalcade start for the mines. Twenty-three horses were waiting, seven of them with ladies' saddles for Lady Glasgow, Lady Augusta Boyle, Lady Kintore, Lady Hilda, and Lady Ethel Keith Falconer, Hilda, and me.

We were accompanied by the gentle-men of our party, and various official people ; the Mayor of Westport headed the cavalcade. You never saw such a miscellaneous collection of animals, as had been lent by all sorts of people, and had come from all parts.

Lady Glasgow chose a quiet pony, as she did not much enjoy the prospect of climbing precipices with her feet dangling over the side. Her son was mounted on a racehorse that was the winner of several cups. I had a stout cob, which I chose because the saddle looked so comfortable.

The doctor from Westport nearly came to grief, as his horse shied at a man who was mending the road, and he was as nearly as possible shot over the cliff. Mr. G——, who is short of stature, was perched on an enormous cart-horse, and was carrying a large white umbrella for one of the ladies. The variety of costumes was extremely amusing, and for the first half-hour we did nothing but go into peals of laughter at each other's appearance.

We rode for an hour and a half up a

zigzag path cut through the thick bush, and under beautiful old trees of red pine, white pine, black birch, and every kind of lovely shrub, some covered with scarlet berries; tree ferns tossing their graceful tops to the blue sky. A lovely little white orchid was brought to me with a delicious scent. We also saw tufts of a plant, with bright blue poison-ous berries, growing on the steep banks. Occasionally the song of the bell-bird, or the Tui, reached us from the tops of the giant trees. One caught glimpses of the sea, far, far away through the trunks, and every turn brought fresh beauties to admire. Each little torrent that ran down the mountain side was bridged by planks, over which the horses had to go; sometimes a noisy little water-fall thundering down close by, bordered by varieties of graceful ferns. I have dried a few specimens of one of these called the umbrella fern. It is so bewildering to make the acquaintance of so many new plants and birds.

We were quite sorry to reach the top, but the excellent lunch that awaited us was very acceptable, after which several speeches were made by the directors, and healths drunk.

The miners' houses are all wooden shanties, built on the bare clearing, with no sort of attempt at smartness or gardens. They look dreadfully squalid and untidy, but in this beautiful climate I think people care less for ornament as long as they have the necessaries of life. All the children looked very healthy and nicely dressed.

We went to see the small loaded trucks arrive from the mine full of coal. They flew along a little tramway, and were emptied down a shoot into the larger trucks. Then we saw the large trucks start down the hill. It took one's breath away to think that any one had actually gone down in them. We perched ourselves on various perilous positions on the rocks at the sides of the cutting, where we could get a good view. The panorama of the country was very fine from that height, stretching away to the faint line of breakers on the sea-coast. We were taken to see the engine-room, and before leaving the little town, Lady Glasgow asked the schoolmaster for a holiday for the children.

They all assembled to see us mount our various steeds, and the descent began. I led the procession, and on reaching the foot we found tea ready for us at the station.

The children of Waimangaroa were all

cheering like mad, headed by their school-mistress, who shouted, "Three cheers for Lady Glasgow, three cheers for the Duchess of B——," as the train moved off; and we had bouquets presented to us by some very small ones.

We saw several Maori hens in the bush; they are rather like hen pheasants, and live on rats, mice, and small birds. Also some green paroquets, which fly about in pairs, their green plumage flashing like emeralds in the sunshine.

On Wednesday, the 15th February, we started for the coaching tour from Westport to Nelson. Lord Glasgow, Lady Augusta, Miss H——, Captain Clayton, Mr. G——, Hilda, and I. Lady Glasgow was prevented coming on account of Alice having caught a severe cold.

We took leave of Lady Kintore and

her daughters, who remained on the *Hinemoa*, and went by sea with the rest of the party to Nelson, where they left by train for Wellington, and thence back to Adelaide *viâ* Sydney. The two coaches, one scarlet, with five white horses, and the other green, with bays, to take the servants and luggage, drove up to the pier, and we all packed in, or rather on the top. I had a seat beside the driver, Mr. Mitchell, a Scotsman, who gave us much information as we went along about the country. The road wound through the valley of the Buller River, a most exciting drive, as there was a precipice sheer down into the foaming torrent on one side, and just room for a coach, and very few places where you could have passed another vehicle.

After the first few miles we drove straight down a steep track, which seemed to land in the bed of the river, which was very wide and free from rocks at this point. Then we discovered that the whole coach had to drive on to a ferry boat, which was worked with ropes, and was pulled across the stream. The horses seemed quite accustomed to it, and stood quiet. We waited at the other side to see the green coach come over.

Unfortunately this day's journey was much spoilt by the rain, which fell very persistently, and blotted out much of the finest part of the scenery. The mountains, covered with thick bush, rose almost perpendicularly from the river's bed, and the road we travelled by was cut out of the side of the hill. The bridges over the torrents were, in most cases, devoid of side rails, which made them very dangerous in case of accident or a horse slipping.

The first stage was 26½ miles to Inangahua Junction, but an hour before reaching it we were invited to stop at a station and have some tea and peaches and cream—a delicious little repast prepared by some people of the name of Walker, two elderly bachelor brothers and a young niece. She had got out all the best china, and after nearly a month at sea, drinking out of real china cups was quite a treat, instead of the heavy things half an inch thick one has to put up with on board ship. Such peaches as we had I have never seen equalled.

·However, we had not much time to linger, and were soon hurried away from this hospitable board, and packed up on the coach to complete our stage.

We lunched at Courtenay's Hotel, all prettily decorated with long tree ferns in our honour—a crowd of school children, as usual, in the foreground. The food at these small inns was generally very nicely cooked, with plenty of good vegetables and fruit—grapes, plums, apples, pears, and bananas, huge apple pies or stewed apricots, and fresh milk and excellent cream. Some men were collected in the veranda, and among them was a most amusing French labourer, who was delighted to have some conversation in his native tongue.

When we started he proposed three extra cheers for " de ladies," and the landlord fired a gun off. Likewise a German miner, who had not spoken German for ten years, and was one of the earliest settlers in the district.

The second stage was eleven miles to Lyell, an " alpine village," as the inhabitants called it. Here we were received with flags flying and cheers from the population, who all turned out, in spite of the rain, to welcome the Governor and hear an address read to him. Wet and weary, we had all to stand in the street till it was over. Some of these addresses were beautifully illuminated.

How glad we were to have a fire in our small parlour, and dry our wet things! The other coach not having arrived, we had to sit in our petticoats, drying our skirts, hats, and boots. A tremendous storm of wind and rain lasted all night. One felt as if the house were coming down, but all slept soundly in comfortable beds—an agreeable change from our narrow berths on board the yacht.

Thursday, 16*th*.—Left Lyell after breakfast. Had a lovely drive, in pretty good weather, of twenty-seven miles, to Longford Accommodation House, kept by our driver Mitchell, who had sent for his wife and baby, etc., to receive us.

They came from a place seventy miles off. The house was all repapered for our reception, and a cheerful wood fire burning in the parlour, in one of the wide brick fire-places one generally finds in these Colonial farm-houses.

We passed a good many small clearings by the Hope River that day, and also drove through much forest scenery. The road was in many places bordered by high bracken, under which there is excellent grass for cattle, as the sun does not get at it to scorch the grass.

Longford is close to the river, and we all walked to see a rope cage, by which means you can get across, that is to say, if it happens to be on the side you arrive at. Hilda was adventurous enough to try it, and so was Augusta. It certainly did look most dangerous and impossible for any one who had not a very steady head, as the cage swings about seventy feet above the bed of the river.

We also went to see the Elephant Rock. It is in the midst of the stream, and looks exactly like an elephant wading in the water, with its long trunk. Another rock is called the Calf. All along this road we had constantly to go through the dry beds of torrents, and got well bumped about in the coach. Elsewhere we went cantering along with the five horses and heavy coach, and the clever way they turned the sharp corners was perfectly marvellous.

We passed a couple of coach wheels on the side of a very steep place. " That," said the driver, " was all that was left of a coach that fell over the side lately, and that mare " (pointing to one of our leaders) " is the only survivor of the team !"

On *Friday, 17th February*, we started

at nine o'clock from Longford, and, after we were all settled on the coach, a photograph was taken of the party. Mrs. Mitchell was very anxious to have the baby in it, but as he began to jump about at the critical moment he was banished. However, I had found him being photoed in the back-yard, in his little chemise, before breakfast, surrounded by different members of the family, chirping and making all sorts of attractive noises that babies are supposed to like ; so, as he had been done justice to already, it was just as well not to have him in our group. We passed the Elephant Rock, and drove by the Owen River, the Hope, and the Matupiko, for about forty miles, and did not stop for lunch till nearly three o'clock. We *were* famished when we drove up to Thompson's Accommodation House, where the usual hearty meal awaited us. Then sixteen miles over a grand mountain range to Bellgrove Station, where we were invited to tea at the engine-driver's house while waiting for our special train in which Lady Glasgow, and her party, came from Nelson to welcome us, so we did the last twenty-two miles of the journey very swiftly.

On reaching Nelson, far from resting from our fatigues, we were received by the Mayor and other swells, and put into open carriages and driven through the town. The artillery fired a salute as the train stopped, and a brass band began to play.

At a foot pace we went through the streets, and the rest of what we did you will see in the newspaper. Slept that night on board the *Hinemoa*.

On *Saturday*, 18*th*, we were all invited to a picnic, given by the Mayor of Nelson, and had a most lovely drive to

Cable Bay, where we inspected the cable station and all the testing instruments, which were most interesting, but extremely difficult to understand. Sent various messages home to say we were well and enjoying ourselves. Some of the girls wanted to have their names telegraphed, as the messages come out on a line of tape, but the clerk at Sydney cabled he was very hungry and just going to his dinner.

We lunched on the banks of a very pretty trout stream, where some lovely brown trout were disporting themselves, but declined to be caught, although several fishers tried their luck. Weather most beautiful, and such a sunset over the harbour!

On *Sunday, 19th,* went to morning service at the Cathedral, a large church built of wood, very well situated at the end of the principal street, and up several flights of steps.

On *Monday*, 20*th*, left Nelson Harbour for Picton. Six hours of very rough sea, and a little misery in the cabin! On landing we proceeded to a goods-shed, where addresses were presented to his Excellency, and bouquets to Lady Glasgow and me. School children sang, and the crowd pressed closer and closer till we were nearly stifled.

The *Rotorua* anchored alongside of us, and began to use our deck as a landing-stage, and to unship her cargo across our bows. The noise and discomfort was so great that I retreated with my maid to an hotel in the town, where I took a room for the night. Lord and Lady Glasgow went to a dinner given by the Mayor.

On *Tuesday*, 21*st*, we all went to the

town of Blenheim for the day by rail, where a great reception awaited us ; but the show was rather spoilt by the rain. Lunch in the Town Hall, and speeches. On our return we went to tea with the Mayor of Picton at his charming villa overlooking the harbour, and were introduced to various members of his family, one of whom confided to me that we were not nearly such alarming persons as she anticipated. We weighed anchor that night about 12 P.M., and started for Wellington.

Wednesday, 22nd. — Anchored for breakfast and packing at the Heads at the entrance of the harbour, a fine sunny day for our first view of Wellington, but desperately windy. The younger Boyle children rushed down to the pier, slap through the crowd to welcome their parents, and sprang into the carriage, and nearly strangled their mother by the vehemence of their embraces.

Later in the day I went for a lovely ride with Eddie and Mr. G—— to Lyell Bay, where we met Hilda and Augusta in the pony cart, and had an enchanting gallop on the sands. The horses were much in want of exercise, and very fresh. I rode a charming animal called Fly.

Thursday, 23rd.—Very showery. Went shopping in the town ; small dance in the evening. There is a delightful, polished floor in the ball-room, which opens out of the drawing-rooms, and is always ready for these festivities. Government House is extremely comfortable, built of wood, with a tower and red roof. All the houses in Wellington are wooden ones, and fires are frequent ; the fire-bell rings instantly to warn the firemen, who fly to the rescue. They are all built rather low, with verandas, and the hills come so close down to the sea that you see funny little dwellings perched in all sorts of extraordinary places just where there is room for a house. The new Government buildings are rather handsome, with pointed gables, and almost adjoin Government House, which stands in a garden full of lovely trees, ferns, flowers, and creepers, with a tennis ground in the rear. The drives all round are very pretty, with peeps across the bay to the distant mountains.

Saturday, 25th.—Lord and Lady Hopetoun, accompanied by Lord Northesk (A.D.C.) and Mr. Ralston, arrived from Picton in the *Hinemoa*, after a very rough passage. I went down with Lord Glasgow to welcome them. It was most amusing to meet them again and exchange experiences of our travels. They are very delighted to have their holiday. A mail is going, so I must stop. I send this from Geyser Hotel, Whakarewarewa, but have not time to write up to date—13th March 1893.

ON THE BANKS OF A TROUT-STREAM, "THE HAPPY VALLEY," NEAR NELSON.

LETTER No. 9.

STEAM-SHIP "MARIPOSA,"
PACIFIC OCEAN, OFF SAMOA,
Wednesday, 29th March 1893.

THIS is a most confusing week, as we
have had two Mondays, by order of the
captain, to get straight.   I must hark back
to 27th February, just after Lord and
Lady Hopetoun arrived at Government
House, Wellington, in the *Hinemoa*.   We

had a very pleasant time there. I painted a good deal, and finished up sketches made in the sounds; prowled in the town, and bought several water-colours and a little oil painting of the Stirling Falls in Milford Sound at sunset.

Some of the party played exciting games of tennis in the garden, and it was delightful sitting under the trees, with all the children and the dogs and pet parrot watching them exerting themselves. The grounds are not large for the size of the house, but full of beautiful trees, shrubs, and tree ferns, and gay flower beds on very green turf. Over and over again we used to say, " Well, this is delightful, considering the frost, and snow, and fogs that everybody at home is suffering from."

On *Wednesday, 1st March*, a large and merry party, consisting of the Hopetouns, five young Boyles, four A.D.C.'s, Hilda, and I, packed into a huge brake with four horses, and started on a twenty miles' drive to a fishing hut on a trout stream at Wainuiomata. The road was a very beautiful one, winding for miles along the sea-shore,—such a blue sea, with a view of mountains, which we gradually reached and began to ascend, some of the party getting out to walk up the steepest parts. I was on the box, and of course heard all about the horses from the driver, who was vexed he had not had longer notice, and was obliged to put a mare in as leader who had not filled that post before.

Considering what a dangerous road it was, I should have been very sorry to drive a team one was not sure of. However, our whip was quite equal to the occasion, and the only misadventure that befell us was that, when we arrived and the horses were unharnessed and turned loose to find their own way down to the stream, two of them made their escape, and wandered several miles into the bush. It took the driver, Lord Northesk, and Mr. Ralston some time to retrieve them, and we were pretty late in getting home. We put a basket full of soda-water and lemonade to cool in the stream, and of course that was the very place the horses selected to drink at. Shrieks from the company, for, in our anxiety, we almost heard all the bottles crashing, and expected a bloody hoof to emerge from the water. However, the first horse just managed to save its distance, and the others were persuaded to try their luck elsewhere. I will not tell you how many trout were caught, as, after driving a coachload of ardent fishermen and women so far, the least we could have expected was a heavy basket, but, alas! alas! "hope told a flattering tale," and we were very glad that a substantial luncheon had been provided by *the management*, and we were not dependent for food on the results of the sport.

On *Thursday, 2nd March*, I paid a visit to the convent schools of St. Mary, and was received by the Mother Superior and her nuns and the priests. Some music was played and songs sung by the pupils; and one very little girl of five recited in a marvellous manner. It was a piece in which she pretended to be a captive bird, and the way she threw up her little arms and looked up with her blue eyes, saying, " I fly, I fly, I pierce the skies," was most dramatic.

The whole scene, when we marched into the school-room with the good nuns, was like a picture by one of the old Dutch masters. A long desk was placed down the centre of the room; on one side sat

the boarders in their Sunday frocks of
sober black, with white lace collars turned
down ; opposite them were the day pupils
in white chiefly, and all graduated according to ages.   By the piano sat one of the
sisters, and several others were grouped
about ; while a row of arm-chairs were
placed at the upper end of the room for
us and the Mother Superior. Some lovely
bouquets were then presented to us, and
afterwards we were taken to see the
chapel. All the running border decora-
tions were painted by the sisters—passion-
flowers, lilies, and vines. Then upstairs
to the dormitories, and down to the kitchen,
each sister in charge being presented.

It is always safe in the Colonies to ask
people what part of the old country they or
their families come from ; and if one happens
to have been near or at their own particular
home spot, they are generally so delighted,

whether in England, Scotland, or Ireland. One sister was in charge of the lace-work done in the convent. It was chiefly tambour-work or net for cheap altar-covers, and a little linen lace.

In the evening Lady Glasgow had a reception in honour of the Governor of Victoria, Lady Hopetoun, and me, as all the Wellington people were very anxious to see us. I put on my best frock, a white and gold brocade, and we all made ourselves as smart as possible. It felt quite odd to be dressing up again after so many weeks of shirts and skirts in the yacht. A mass of people were presented, and all the rest of the time I was in Wellington I felt dreadfully afraid of cutting some one I was supposed to know. This party was rather an ordeal: whenever one looked up, rows and rows of eyes gazing at one. We enjoyed the small after-dinner dances much more, as they were less formal. Being Lent, they could not have a big ball.

Colonel Pitt, who was one of the party at the Mayor of Nelson's picnic to Cable Bay, sent me some charming platinotype photos he had taken of Cable Bay, and the *Hinemoa* steaming out of Nelson Harbour.

On *Friday, 3rd March*, we were invited to a picnic by Sir Patrick Buckley, to see the beautiful scenery on the Wainarapa Railway. The carriages are provided with a balcony along the side, where you can stand, enclosed with wire netting, feeling like a sheep in a sheep-truck, and admire the rapidly-dissolving views. We went up the Rimataku Incline, and past the place where a train was blown over in a gale of wind. Since then strong barriers have been put up at this exposed bridge to prevent the recurrence of such a disaster. Five people were killed and others hurt.

We went as far as a station called Pigeon's Bush, where we had a sumptuous lunch, and heaps of delicious grapes. I did a hasty sketch of blue mountains, with some cabbage-trees for foreground ; but one might have spent weeks on that lovely line, painting at every turn, and it was simply maddening only to be able to take such very inadequate sketches of so much that was extremely grand and beautiful. In the evening there was again a small dance at Government House, the Governor and Lord Hopetoun taking part in a vigorous reel of Tulloch.

On *Saturday, 4th March*, left Wellington and our kind and hospitable entertainers at 6.30 A.M., in company with the Hopetouns and their staff, as far as

Waipukurau, where my cousins, Mr. and Mrs. Montgomery, were waiting to meet us with a buggy and two nice grays. We had breakfast in the train dining-car, where they cooked chops—oh! so hot—in a small kitchen compartment, and gave us paper napkins, which were very funny, covered with pink advertisements. At one of the stations we passed some Maori ladies, riding astride, dressed in gay cottons with coloured handkerchiefs on their heads. The train passed through the Manawatu Gorge; but the day was cloudy, showery, and windy, so we did not see it to advantage. After many adieus to our fellow-travellers at Waipukurau Station, we collected our luggage and many bags, cushions, rugs, sticks, and sketching-boards, and proceeded to the Tavistock Hotel, about a mile or two from the station, kept by a Scotchman of the name of Gow, who, with his obliging wife did his best to make our stay comfortable.

We found that Harry Montgomery had taken all the rooms, and they had come down from their wooden cottage at the Run to entertain us during our stay. As it was about 3.30, we did not do much that evening except rest and recover from our fatigues.

Next day, *Sunday, 5th March*, I walked to church with my cousins and little Mary; service done by a lay reader, who preached a peculiar sermon on electric lighting and other modern improvements. In the afternoon we drove by the banks of the Tuki Tuki River. At one point the road was actually in the bed of part of the river, which in winter is a tremendous torrent. There had been some rain, so our road was occasionally under water; huge plants of toi grass met overhead, and quantities of native flax grew with it. We spent all afternoon exploring and sketching a lovely view of the great range of the Ruahine Mountains.

On *Monday, 6th*, we were taken to Woburn and Hatuma; lunched in the three-roomed wooden cottage, where the Montgomerys are staying for the summer, although they mean to move later into the manager's house. I did an oil sketch of the homestead for Maude, under the shade of an umbrella tied to a wheelbarrow, and Hilda sketched me in this absurd position. Later, we saddled all the horses and rode out on the Run; miles and miles of grass, with occasional cabbage-trees, especially on one place where there is good soil, called "cabbage-tree flat." We were also taken to see the wool-shed, which must present a busy scene when full of Maori shearers and their wives, sorting the fleeces, and handing them to be pressed in bundles for sale. The weather was lovely, and we were sorry when the riding was over, saddles taken off, and the grays put in the buggy ; Harry and little Mary escorted us riding. Quite a bush road, or rather a bullock track, as far as the manager's house at Woburn. There are a good many old weeping-willow trees about, and in the avenue all along the banks of the stream. They are a very general feature in New Zealand scenery, and were originally brought from St. Helena. In the hall at Tavistock Hotel were several splendid stags' heads : the red deer thrive well, and grow to an immense size. Quite recently one was killed with twenty-two points. The heads are far finer than any I have seen in the Highlands of Scotland. Mr. Gow presented me with a stick carved by

Maories—one of those creeper sticks that have been eaten into by the parasite creeper as it twines round. He gave Hilda the tusks of a wild boar, which abounds in some parts of the bush, and gives very good sport. Two men killed eighty pigs in three days.

On *Tuesday 7th*, we spent most of the day sketching on the Tuki Tuki River; taking lunch with us, unharnessing the horses, and tying them to flax bushes.

Wednesday, 8th, drove with Maude past a Maori pah, and on to a small town, where we got some milk at the hotel, and I sketched a picture in the hall of the half-caste daughter of a Maori chief.

Afterwards in the garden of a hut we saw two Maori women washing, and an old man who remembered Maude's father, Mr. Russel, and said, " He was my father."

The women were tatooed with green on their lips and chins, the colour of green-stone, which they so much admire. At first one thinks it hideous and most disfiguring, but after we had been at the hot lakes, and seen so many at the Maori settlement, we got used to it, and a Maori woman seemed quite unfinished without green lips.

We left for Napier by the two o'clock train, a three hours' broiling journey, the train quite full—men, women, and babies in profusion; one lovely baby with golden curls all over its head and pink cheeks. Of course, this time we were not travelling with a Governor and his staff, so had to make the best of it.

On reaching Napier we found a fine open carriage waiting to take us to the hotel.

We went to a chocolate shop, and bought some boxes by way of provision for the morrow. Walked a little way on the fine esplanade, of which the town is very proud, but having had plenty of the sea lately, we did not stop long to admire the waves breaking.

Next morning, *9th March*, we started at eight o'clock in a private buggy, driven by a nice young Irishman called Brady, who gave us a lot of information as we went along. Our road lay all along by the Inner Harbour for some miles, and in the calm water all the rocks and headlands were reflected most beautifully. Then we went through the fertile valley of the Petane, and began to ascend the Titiokuru Range (2750 feet). Stopped at Mohaka to lunch and change horses. The scenery was most beautiful and interesting. The road ascended to the top of Turanga-kumu (3500 feet), from which there was a fine panorama.

We soon began to descend the famous

zigzag (4¾ miles) to Stone Creek; then past the Waipunga Creek, and arrived at dusk at Tarawera, where we met all the coaching travellers, and dined with them at a sort of table d'hôte in the kitchen. Our bed-rooms were little attics, with sloping roofs and casement windows.

On *Friday*, 10*th*, up early for our forty-six mile drive. Alas! it was a pouring wet day, and we missed a good deal of the beauty of the road in consequence. We crossed the Kaingaroa Plains, saw several herds of wild horses, and stopped at Rangitaiki Hotel for lunch, where a charming and compassionate landlady helped us to dry our clothes at a wood fire.

As the only luggage with us was carried in bags, which had got soaked through, we had to unpack them and spread our garments to dry. In so doing some of them got singed, and poor Miss James was especially exasperated over a new red silk shirt she had just made for me, with a multitude of little tucks. It was bad enough to get it wet, but worse to get it singed, after all her labour over these little tucks. I am afraid we were more inclined to laugh over our misfortunes, and her tragic face added to our amusement. At last, having arrayed ourselves in some partially dry petticoats, we returned to our buggy, much pitied by the coach passengers, who thought themselves so much better off in that bumpy vehicle, because they could draw all the leather curtains round and sit tight, like pigeons in a pie. The constant rain became monotonous, and after passing Opepe, a point of historic interest in the Maori war, Hilda persuaded Mr. Brady that it would be safe for her to take the reins for a bit. This he very un-

wisely consented to do and took a back
seat himself. The result of the manœuvre
was disastrous, when we began to descend a
small hill. The horses were accustomed
to have the drag put on, but this lady-
driver had made herself comfortable with a
thick rug over her feet, and when the
critical moment came she could not find
the skid, and of course the buggy touched
a horse's hocks, and he began to kick.
The other horse, seeing an opportunity for
mischief, threw his head up and made a
plunge, nearly dragging the reins out of
the driver's hands, and almost pulling her
slender person right out of the seat. We
had some work to get them pulled up, and
were already off the road, bumping over
stones and grass tussocks. We lost one
of the bolts of the cross-bar, and broke my
umbrella ; James had hers caught by the
wind and turned inside out. Fortunately

we were all more shaken than hurt. We all hopped out and walked in the wet, till the road was level, and the horses had calmed down from their excitement. "No more amateur driving of bush horses for me, if you please," was my stern mandate. We missed the fine views of Tongariro and Ngaruhoe and Mount Ruapehu (5578 feet), as they were enveloped in mist. Reached Taupo, well soaked again, and thankful to sit over the fire in the sitting-room, and go early to bed. There were a number of Maories at Taupo, but the bad weather prevented them from dancing the haka, and we were sorry to miss the opportunity of seeing a spontaneous exhibition of their national dances.

On *Saturday*, 14*th*, had a twenty-five mile drive. Stopped at Ateamuri for lunch, where was a lovely view of river and a great rocky hill standing up in the plain,

on the top of which was a Maori pah at
the time of the war.   A pah means a sort
of fortified stockade ; but now they speak
of a settlement as a Maori pah, which is
not correct.   This hill is called " Poha-
turoa," which means " Long Stone."   The
day gradually cleared up, and was fine
towards afternoon.   We passed the great
Horohoro Range (2500 feet), from which
stands out Hinemoa's Rock ; entered the
Hemo Gorge, and soon came to a fine
view of Rotorua and its lake.   Then we
descended a winding road to Whakarewarewa, where we drew up at the Geyser
Hotel, and saw various figures on the
veranda making violent signs of welcome.
They were the Hopetouns, Baron Luttwitz,
Mr. Featherston, Lord Northesk, and Mr.
Ralston, who were all starting for their
evening bathe at the hot springs, with
towels over their arms.   How delighted

we were to meet again at this out of the world spot! and after our long cramping drives, it was delicious to go down to the bathing-houses and float about in the warm sulphur baths. We passed the pool where the Maories bathe all together in the open air. Such a lot of brown satin skins and black heads bobbing about! They sit in the pool up to their necks, and laugh and talk the whole time. We used to have long conversations with them, Sophia, the Maori guide, acting as interpreter. She is a half-caste, and in her youth must have been very pretty; and although she has been twice married, and has children and grandchildren, she wears wonderfully, and still possesses quantities of long black hair, only a little gray at the temples. I did her portrait, which you shall see, and also drew several sketches of the other women washing and sitting on their heels. They were pleased that we sat also on the ground when we wished to converse with them, and told Sophia " they were sure " I was " a great chief," as they could see I was not ashamed to talk to them.

One poor woman had a very bad hand ; in some quarrel another woman had bitten her thumb and broken the bone. With their usual fear of doctors, who would perhaps cut it off, and thereby prevent her from having the use of the injured limb in the next world, nothing had ever been done, and the hand was in a fearful state. I tried to persuade them to send her to the doctor at Rotorua, and told the hotel-keeper about it, so I trust something was done for her relief.

I heard of another case of a poor Maori who got his arm badly crushed. He was taken to the hospital, but would not hear of having it amputated without his father's consent, although every hour, in the opinion of the surgeons, was valuable in case 'mortification should set in. The old father flew into a fearful rage when he was consulted, and said that his son would want his arm in the next world, and it was better for him to die with it and keep it, as it couldn't be sent after him. The extraordinary part of it was that the man recovered. His arm is quite useless, but he still keeps it.

These worthy people cook all their food in the hot springs. I saw the chief's wife, in a scarlet dress, cooking one day. She had a little plaited basket in the water, and into it she was throwing small pieces of dough. Another woman had a piece of pig and some potatoes in a string basket. It looked rather nasty, and I do not think I should like to see them eating it, as it is generally a case of fingers were made before forks.

Sophia has an old relative she calls " Auntie." This old, old woman is a chief's daughter, and rejoices in the name of Hangaiate Rangitantini, but in the settlement she is generally called Cup-o-tea. She afforded us a great deal of entertainment. Her hair is cut short, as is their custom for mourning; in one ear she wears the head and beak of a huia, and in the other a long greenstone ear-ring. A short white shirt, and still shorter petticoat, complete her costume. When she wishes to be very smart, she puts on a brilliant tartan shawl, sky blue and scarlet, with bars of yellow, being the prevailing tints.

Alas ! the picturesque cloaks of native flax with curious borders are quite gone out ; the people are so lazy, they will not take the trouble to prepare the flax and the native dyes.

Old Cup-o-tea is the only one in the settlement who still works diligently. Baron Luttwitz bought from her a lovely little cloak, but he had hard work to get her to part with it. Hilda made great friends with the old lady. One day, when she was in particular good humour, she turned out all the possessions in her hut to rummage for some " huia " feathers, which she presented to Hilda, and consented also to sell her greenstone ear-ring. Sophia and I also exchanged tokens of affection.

One evening we were in our little sitting-room, when the Baron opened the door, and said, "A queen is coming to visit you." The door opened, and in walked Sophia, dressed in a long white Maori cloak, covered with black tags, a couple of long huia feathers in her hair, and a wonderful greenstone ornament round her neck. We ordered some whisky for her, and soon started her on the subject of the great earthquake,—a most interesting story, and perfectly terrible it must have been for those who were present, when the great mountain, Tarawera, was burst open, and the whole air filled with stones and fire-balls, succeeded by a fall of ashes, in which several villages were smothered and many people killed.

Sophia lived at that time at Wairoa, one of the doomed settlements, as she was guide to the wonderful pink and white terraces which were then destroyed.

She told us that a phantom canoe was seen the previous afternoon, not only by her and other natives, but also by some of the tourists, with whom she was rowing back by the lake. At first there were thirteen people seen in it, then fewer and fewer, till only one was left, as the canoe glided behind a rock and disappeared. This was considered a very bad omen. Sophia inhabited a very substantial and well-built "warrie," as their houses are called. She sheltered about forty natives on that dreadful night, when the roofs of other native huts were stove in.

The schoolmaster's family had a terrible time of it. At first they were delighted with the splendid view of the eruption from their veranda, and stood outside looking at it. Everybody seems to have done that at first for a couple of hours, instead of making their escape. When the ashes began to fall, it got quite dark and was too late. They lit the fire in their stove, as a piercing wind began to blow, and then they were nearly suffocated by the smoke coming down the chimney.

When the roof began to give way,

the mother was sitting in the middle of
the room by the stove with her three
younger children by her, the little girl on
her knee. They got wedged down by a
beam, and could not move ; the mother
was many hours after dug out by the search
party, but the children were dead. The
eldest girl, her father, and a friend, contrived to break a window they were
standing near, and so escaped into the
paddock, where they stumbled about
amongst fallen trees till they reached the
hen-house ; there they took refuge for the
night. Another child and its Maori nurse
were discovered alive under a wash-hand
stand in the bedroom.

At early dawn everybody who could,
made their way through the bush to Whakarewarewa, the track often obstructed by
fallen trees. Half-way they were met by
the hotel-keeper and his coach, who drove

the terror-stricken fugitives to a place of safety; but the men returned to search for the missing and buried people in the huts and houses.

One young English tourist lost his life, and a monument has been erected to his memory.

On *Sunday*, 12*th March*, I got up very early to see the Hopetouns start in their red coach, Hopetoun and Mr. Ralston riding. They were bound for Canterbury, and we were dreadfully sorry they could not stay longer to explore the country in our company. Baron Luttwitz escorted us to church, and we also inspected the Maori tribal meeting-house at Rotorua. It was beautifully carved, with monsters in red all along the dado; and at the upper end of the building was a sort of railed off altar on which stands a bust of Queen Victoria.

I am told the Maories bow before it, and even pray there.

An old, old native woman and a stalwart youth fought for the shilling we paid at the door. A whole family were encamped in one corner, playing "nap" for matches. This seems to be a favourite amusement. The outside of the house was beautifully carved, and ornamented with shells and red paint. In the afternoon we went nine miles across the lake in a little steam-launch, landed, and were rowed by Maories up a river, to see its source, which bubbles in a cold spring straight out of the ground. We could row right up the stream till we reached this cul-de-sac. We threw coppers in to see them fly up again by the force of the water. It was a most curious sight. The lake was rather rough coming back, and we had not time to land on the island in the middle, where a tribe of natives live, and see Hinemoa's bath, and the rest of the settlement.

Hinemoa was the daughter of a chief, and being separated from her lover, heard the sound of his lute one evening over the water. She plunged into the lake and swam across to his island, and took refuge in the bath. When an old slave came with a calabash for water, she took it from him and broke it; he returned with another, which Hinemoa broke again. The third time the young chief came down in wrath and discovered her, and took her to wife, and their descendants are still among the tribe. So runs the legend. Such a lovely sunset, the hills changing from blue to gold, and from gold to deep violet, and all the hues reflected in the water.

On *Monday*, 13*th March*, we hired some

hacks, and Hilda, Baron Luttwitz, and I rode ten miles to the buried village of Wairo. It was a lovely expedition—first a few miles along the flat moor, then ascending a delicious lane, where the branches met overhead,—a beautiful piece of bush scenery, which has reclothed itself with verdure since the eruption. Birds were singing in the branches, and sunlight streaming through the skeletons of giant trees on beautiful fairy tree-ferns and creepers and bracken, higher than our horses' heads. Once or twice we had to turn aside from the path, and make a detour on account of the deep chasms caused by the earthquake across the road. Formerly coaches went that way every day, but now, in places, it was hard enough to find footing for one horse, the land having slipped and crumbled away till a tiny ledge was all that was left.

We emerged from the woods on a lovely view of Lake Tikitapu ; galloped along its white pebbly shore ; followed another adventurous path by the side of the mountains that rise straight from the beach ; crossed the shoulder of a hill, and came in sight of Lake Rotokakahi ; and so on to Wairoa—its ruined huts and poor mill-wheel half buried in volcanic ashes, presenting a most melancholy spectacle. The hotel was a mass of ruin. Two men were there who had tied up their horses, and were exploring about—one was the photographer from Rotorua, and the other a Government inspector of roads. They pointed out the schoolmaster's house and Sophia's " warrie."

We continued to ride on, but were rather sorry we had not tied up our horses with the others, as the road suddenly ceased, and we got on to a sort of ploughed field of ashes, partly covered with high ferns and scrub, ending in precipices straight down to Lake Tarawera. In the distance we saw Mount Tarawera illuminated by a brilliant gleam of sun.

At last we came to a chasm, and had all to get off and make the horses jump down, and then found we could not proceed with them any farther; so we tied their reins under their off fore-legs, and left them to amuse themselves with the herbage while we scrambled on. I found a capital foreground for a sketch—a huge rock with skeleton trees on it, and the lake and mountain behind. As usual, when one begins to sketch, the most aggravating thing happens—the only shower of rain we had all day just began and spotted all my paper, and of course we had left our capes with the horses. It didn't last long, and we had a lovely ride home. We picked up a little scrap of carved leg of chair or something from one of the ruined houses as a memento.   Half-way home we met two Maori boys on horseback ; they had been sent to see if we were all safe, as Mrs. Nelson had worked herself into a state on account of the danger of the road, and had been upbraiding her husband for letting us go without a guide.

When we were about two miles from the settlement some magnificent thunder-clouds we had been watching began to burst in a storm of heavy rain.   We hurried up our steeds and galloped as hard as we could, to the delight of the Maori boys, to whom anything in the shape of a race is a joy ; and before getting thoroughly drenched we scampered into the hotel en-closure, and dismounted at the veranda, under the amused supervision of the other travellers, who had been watching our head-

THE BRAIN POT, WHAKAREWAREWA.

To face p. 203.

long course with interest and our efforts to escape the rain-storm.

That morning I had had a perigrination with Sophia round the geysers, and had heard all her stories about the different spots,—such as the Brain-Pot, where a poor chief's head was cooked after he had successfully, for a time, eluded the pursuit of his enemies in a cave she showed me, close to a hot spring called the Chief's Bath.

Two of the principal geysers have periods of great activity, when they play like huge fountains for half-an-hour or so, throwing volumes of boiling water up to a height of seventy feet. When the sun shines on them, making rainbows on the spray, the effect is wonderful, and one sees Sophia like the witch of some giant cauldron, her picturesque figure looming very weirdly through the vapours.

When we were walking up to the settlement we passed her bare-footed, with her dress very much in a *negligé* style. She caught hold of Baron Luttwitz, and implored him to ask me to look the other way while she fetched her shoes, as she did not wish to be introduced to me with bare feet! When she returned from her rapid flight to her hut, she had spoiled her appearance by tying a white cloth under her chin, and by putting on a long blue dress and some stout shoes; also arming herself with a stick.

Another day I made a little sketch of her daughter Miriam and her baby "Queenie"—such a little yellow-faced atom, with black eyes. The children used to come and sit in rows, patting their chests and saying, "Me, me," wishing to be immortalised. We wound up the day by a delicious bath.

On *Tuesday*, 14*th*, we hired Mr. Nelson's spider buggy and a reliable horse. Baron Luttwitz accompanied us as outrider, and we also took a side-saddle, so that in case the road was very bad, one of us might take a turn riding. Hilda and I drove in turns, and we had no upset this time; although the horse, by catching the reins with his tail, did his best at critical moments to spoil our journey.

We drove along the shore of the lake to Tikitere, where there are more geysers and hot springs and baths—most primitive ones, shaded by native huts, which are by no means air-tight, being simply constructed of reeds and rushes on a wooden framework. The house of our guide, M‘Croty, was of this description. He is married to the Maori woman to whom the property belongs. She followed us, her grandchild on her back. We stopped to talk to her and praise the beauty of the little half-caste baby. It had lovely roguish eyes and brown hair curling all over its head, but was very spoilt, and would not consent to leave its granny's arms in order to allow her to dance us a few steps of the haka for our diversion.

We wandered round the springs with terrible names—Dante's Inferno, the fumes of which were enough to suffocate you; Hell's Gate, a pond of boiling mud, smelling of sulphur and brimstone. One had to follow the guide pretty closely, as a false step or two on the thin crust would have ended in the seething cauldron, from which there is no way out alive. We ascended by some lava terraces the banks of the stream, and crossed it at a waterfall that fell very prettily over the white lava. And making a detour, we ascended a little hill (oh! it was a steep pull in the blazing sun!) from whence we had a lovely view of lakes and mountains.

On *Wednesday*, 18*th* of *March*, we again betook us to the spider buggy, and drove twenty miles in it to Waiotapu. The road wound through a succession of low hills, and was not very interesting till we had almost reached the springs, when a fine view of snow-capped mountains came in sight. After lunching in a Maori hut I started off to paint, accompanied by a tall, handsome Maori youth, son of the guide, and several little boys, who each carried something for me. There was no shade to be found, and I had to do the sketch on my knees, crouching in the heath, tormented by sand-flies. I made one of the boys sit in the foreground. I heard a little shout from one of the others, and looking up saw an old gray horse ambling towards us with a whole family on its back. " Niggers riding," said one of the boys, with a tone of great contempt. We all laughed, the three little black figures looked so funny, and I got them to stop for a moment while I did a hasty sketch ; then it was time to return to the hut. There are several geysers at this place, and a primrose terrace, but not very remarkable ; and I was too tired to go the round with the guide, who had already conducted the rest of the coaching parties, who had come from our hotel.

On the road home we went back a different way for some miles by the Parcheru Slopes, from whence we had a perfectly magnificent view of Mount Tarawera and the eruption district. I was very much annoyed that we had not gone to this place at once and spent the day there, where I could have done a big drawing, as the panorama was much finer than anything we had yet seen, and there was a lovely piece of wild bush that would have made a beautiful foreground.

This detour took us over the very worst road on which we have yet attempted to drive, and I should have been very sorry to try it in anything but a spider buggy.

Coming down from the slopes we spied a herd of wild horses. Baron Luttwitz immediately rode off as hard as he could in pursuit. They all galloped past not very far from us,—a good-looking stallion and several well-bred mares and foals, their long tails and manes flying in the wind.

Thursday, 16*th March*, we devoted to resting and doing small sketches in the settlement.

I walked out at sunset in a direction we had not yet explored, and got some perfectly lovely views of mountains in the fading light.

On *Friday*, 17th, we proceeded on our travels. Left Whakarewarewa at 11 A.M., after many adieux to our Maori friends, and drove in a private buggy to Okororie, through lovely bush scenery and splendid mountains. We stopped once to change horses and have lunch ; also got some tea at a roadmaker's hut, which was all papered from the *Illustrated London News*, *Sporting and Dramatic*, etc. He had a nice wife, who made us welcome, and provided slices of excellent bread and butter ; but I did feel sorry for her living in that poky place swarming with flies ; however, you can't have sunshine without them apparently. She was very proud of her first baby, and had a little sister staying with her who acted as nurse.

A Maori couple were located, as they expressed it, in an adjoining hut ; the woman was dressed in a scarlet cotton garment, and had a good greenstone ear-ring, which, however, no blandishments would induce her to part with. She smoked a short black pipe, and was full of smiles till the subject of her ear-ring was broached. This drive was thirty-five miles.

We reached the hotel at Okororie at sunset, and lost no time in hurrying down to the Fairy Bath, where we had a good swim before dinner. It is a most ideal place to bathe, surrounded by steep banks clothed with beautiful ferns, and a little wooden shed to dress in. The river there is most peculiar; the path to the bath-houses passes along its banks, and the water all suddenly disappears and rushes through a small tunnel in the rocks, at the other side of which it immediately widens into quite a respectable stream. If it had not been such a dark night, the innkeeper (who, by the by, is a Brill man, and was delighted to welcome me) would have given us some fishing, as the stream abounds in excellent trout.

Next morning, *Saturday, 18th March,* we were up and breakfasted by 6 A.M., and off to the railway station in a buggy, a drive of a couple of miles. There we found the Governor's saloon reserved for us, so made the journey in great comfort, reaching Auckland at 2.30. All the Glasgow children met us at the station. We were just in time to say adieu to Lord Hopetoun, who sailed in the *War-rimoo* for Australia that afternoon. He is going a tour in Queensland, but Lady Hopetoun remains at Government House for a fortnight.

On *Sunday, 19th.* went to morning service at St. Mary's Cathedral Church.

Monday, 20th March, we were invited by Colonel and Mrs. Goring (he is commander of the defence force of the district of Auckland) to a tea picnic on the sea-shore, near Lake Takapuna. Hilda and I were staying at the Grand Hotel, but we lived most of the day at Government House. All the party there were included in the invitation, and a very merry crew we were. Horses and carriages were all put on board the ferry-boat, and on reaching the other side we mounted our various buggies and steeds. I rode that delightful horse Fly, and had a splendid gallop along the sands. We found some pretty little shells on the shore, and some of us sketched while the kettle was boiling. A lovely sunset finished the day. The twilight is so short in those latitudes, which makes painting sunsets a very difficult business.

On *Tuesday*, 21*st*, Alice Boyle drove me to the top of Mount Eden in her pony-cart, from which point of vantage you can see the whole town of Auckland and all the coast for miles and miles, with mountains in the distance, everything spread out like a map ; and it is a very easy way of learning the geography of the locality, and quite as good as if you went up in a balloon.   Mount Eden is an extinct volcano, and you can see down into the crater, now covered with good pasture for cattle.

Wednesday, *22nd March*, the grand Savil Cup Tournament of the New Zealand Polo Association commenced at Potter's Paddock.   The following Polo Clubs competed :—Warrengate Polo Club, J. Cameron, captain ; Auckland No. 1 Team, E. D. O'Rorke, captain ; Auckland No. 2 team, H. Wynyard, captain ; Christchurch Polo Club, A. R. G. Rhodes, captain ; Poverty Bay, S. Williamson, captain ; Rangitikei, and Kihikihi.   We all attended, and great was the excitement, everybody present having some personal interest in the players. They have a capital ground and commodious stand.

Thursday, 23rd, was spent in a visit to the famous ostrich farm of Mr. Nathan. It was a twenty-mile drive, but no one thinks twice of these distances in the Colonies. I did enjoy seeing these beautiful birds, and made some hasty drawings of them. It would be quite a new compliment to say to any one, " You have the eye of an ostrich." They really have the most beautiful eyes and eyelashes. We began by inspecting the little chicks and the mother hen ostrich, who was sitting in an outhouse. Then we saw the six-weeks'-old birds, and so on, till we came to the oldest and savagest old cock ostrich. There were about 200 of them altogether, and they were in separate paddocks. Several collie dogs accompanied the manager, and were sent in pursuit of the birds, who came tearing along from the farthest corners of the fields just like a flock of sheep, all their black and white plumes nodding in the breeze. It was the prettiest sight imaginable. We were also shown the plucking-box, where the birds are driven in, one at a time, to be stripped of their valuable wing feathers before they begin to moult. Mrs. Dibble, the manager's wife, made us hospitably welcome at tea : she had a little girl staying with her for country air, whom I sketched in the shed with the female ostrich.

We inspected the room where the feathers are kept in chests for the market, and all the different qualities. One pound of the best white feathers costs £28, and those grey ones, of which you see so many boas made and feather trimmings, are really the plumage of the young ostriches before they turn black and white.

On *Friday, 24th,* Lord and Lady Glasgow arrived in the *Hinemoa* in time for the polo in the afternoon, which was still going on. We were very glad to have a glimpse of them before embarking ourselves that evening after dinner in the *Mariposa.* Lady Glasgow presented the silver cup won by the Christchurch team. Lady Hopetoun and I each threaded a needle in the needle and thread competition. They were really paper-knives, with slits for eyes and ribbon for thread. Captain Hunter Blair (Lady Glasgow's brother) distinguished himself very much on the Auckland side. Young Mr. Rhodes, who travelled out with us in the *Arcadia,* was in the Christchurch team ; he had first-rate ponies and also rode extremely well. We visited them all in the sheds before the play began.

A large contingent from Government

House accompanied us on board—Lady
Hopetoun, the Boyle girls, and Miss
H——. Colonel Pat. Boyle, Captain
Clayton, Lord Northesk, Captain Hunter
Blair, etc. We had secured a good deck
cabin, and expected to be pretty comfort-
able. Colonel Boyle introduced the captain
(Heyward). He and all the officers are
Americans, and all middle-aged people—no
such young officers as on board the *Arcadia*.

We were dreadfully sorry to say good-
bye to all these dear friends, and to think
our happy time was over. They all did
their best to persuade us to prolong our
stay, and the Hopetouns used every conceivable argument to induce us to return
to Melbourne for their winter season.

I must really wind up this lengthy letter,
or you will all be tired of reading it;
so I shall leave the description of our visit
to Samoa and Honolulu till we get on

shore.   Thank goodness that will be in two days, if all goes well. We are heartily sick of the voyage, and the many times my paper has been blown away, and the ink upset, and all the aggravations of writing on board ship repeated, have tried my patience sorely.

I think it is *very noble* of me to try to write this journal, especially as we had a head wind most of the way, and lost twenty hours from rough weather on the voyage.

THE LITTLE GIRL IN THE OSTRICH PEN

LETTER No. 10.

THE ANTLERS HOTEL,
COLORADO SPRINGS, COLORADO. U.S.,
24th April 1893.

My last letter was finished in mid ocean, and posted at San Francisco. Now I must go back to the 30th March. Everybody awoke about 4 A.M. I looked out of my cabin and saw a most lovely range of mountains by moonlight. It was the coast of Samoa. We hurried to dress (no waiting for a turn of the bath that morning), and every one was on deck, rushing about, drinking tea or cocoa, and making hasty meals of dry bread or biscuit ; we were all in such a desperate hurry to get on shore.

After a couple of hours the sun was up, and we were allowed to land. Mr. Haggard, the Commissioner at Samoa, who had been written to by Lady Jersey about us, came to fetch us in his boat, with such a smart awning and splendid native rowers :—

They had dark yellow skins, and curly dark brown hair, and very good features. Mr. Haggard took us to see his house, where Lady Jersey and her daughter lived when they visited the island.

We then walked through the town, and beyond it to a native house, where we all sat cross-legged on mats, while some "kava" was prepared for us by "Tua," the village maiden whose business it is to entertain strangers. She pounded the root of the kava in an oval wooden bowl, with legs carved out of a solid piece of wood; then poured water on it, and served it round in a cocoa-nut cup. Each person poured a drop or two on the ground before drinking, and then said a sentence in Samoan, which we learnt for the moment; it meant "Good health to you" (Manoia).

I asked permission to sketch the village maiden, and also one or two other women who were in the hut. All around were the most beautiful palm-trees and all kinds of shrubs, and natives constantly passing, and children playing about. The beauty of the place is that it is so unspoilt by civilisation, and the native dress is still worn. A piece of tappa cloth, made from the bark of trees, with curious brown and red patterns over it, forms a sort of petticoat ; and the women wear white or blue muslin over the shoulders, and also a girdle with hanging shreds of dyed bark—scarlet, white, and black. I was given one of these girdles ; they are very gay and pretty. On the way back to the ship we passed several native canoes with cargoes of coral for sale : quite large pieces of coral rock, white and pink. They managed their little canoes with great skill, using small black paddles.

Mr. Stevenson, the author, with whose delightful books you are doubtless familiar, lives at Samoa ; he was on board the *Mariposa* with his wife and step-daughter, but so ill most of the voyage that we hardly saw him, which we regretted very much.

The next day everybody suffered somewhat from the effects of their exertions on shore, and perhaps also from the curious drinks of which they had partaken.

On *Saturday, April 1st*, we saw the Great Bear and the Southern Cross together, and on Sunday, 2nd, we crossed the line. Rough weather began, and a head wind and a heavy sea ; huge waves broke over the bows, and rushed down over the decks, and into the scuppers, making us very wet and uncomfortable.

At every moment of the day one was liable to aggravating accidents. For instance, I was trying to get through a cup of cocoa for breakfast, feeling rather bad, and lying down in my deck chair, when the ship gives a worse lurch than usual, and over goes the hot cocoa, soaking me to the skin. Oh! I was disgusted, having just arrayed myself in a clean white blouse. It is a common thing for a glass of wine or a mustard pot to land in people's laps at lunch; and as for the things in one's cabin, they go flying about all over the place.

Going to sleep is a matter of difficulty, as every timber in the ship creaks and strains, and the wind whistles and shrieks in the rigging as if an army of fiends were let loose; and one begins to wonder if one will ever get safe home, or if one is after all destined as food for the fishes.

I never spent a more miserable Easter than on that old ship. We did not have any sort of service on board. They used to have musical evenings in the social hall occasionally, and one lady sang beautifully, another Australian girl recited, and another was a great traveller, and related her experiences in China, Alaska, and else-where.

A young man and his friend told me a most interesting story of their shipwreck, in January last, on the coast of Ceylon. They were going from Calcutta to Colombo in the Messagerie S.S. *Niemen.* I will give you the rest in his own words. He said :—

"We were off the north-east coast of Ceylon, thirty miles from Trincomalee, and all was apparently going well. I went down to my cabin to fetch something, when suddenly there was a tremendous jerk, and my water-bottle and tumbler flew out of their places on the washstand on to the floor. I thought nothing of it, fancying the ship had begun to roll, and replaced them. A moment later the same thing happened again ; this time the glasses were broken. I ran up to the saloon, and saw the piano dancing about in an extraordinary way ; so I rushed on deck to see what was the matter, and found every one in a wild state of excitement.

" The propeller had stripped itself of the blades, causing the shaft to run wild ; and snapping the bearings, stove in two plates in the stern, through which the sea began to pour in.   We were about eight miles from the coast.

" The captain was almost beside himself, His order was given for all sail to be hoisted, and we ran for the shore at the rate of one and a half knots an hour. All the passengers collected on deck. Fortunately we reached the coast, and anchored outside the reef, in five fathoms of water, where the breakers were sending up clouds of surf.   Even in a good surf-boat at Madras the landing seems formid-able.   What an outlook it was with all these helpless women and children, as the ship's boats were pretty sure to be upset !

"The captain, instead of landing the passengers in daylight as soon as possible, while the sea was calm, ordered the commissaire, with maps and compasses, to land first and take bearings, and see where we were, as he thought that the ship being anchored in five fathoms of water could not sink beyond the hurricane deck, and that it was safer for passengers to remain aboard. All this time there might have been preparations made in the shape of provisions, etc., and blankets being put in the boats; but nothing was done. Some of these boats had no rudder, and hardly an oar.

"The ship went on sinking, but they decided to serve dinner, which was accordingly done, partly to calm the passengers and inspire them with confidence. Suddenly the water began to pour in at the ports of the dining-saloon, and a rush was made for the deck, some people getting out by the skylights the best way they could. I remained with some other men till the water was up to our waists, hunting for life belts, a lot of which we managed to secure and take on deck. Shortly after an order was shouted that all the passengers (150) were to go on to the bridge and forecastle, as the vessel was settling down much faster and lower than the captain anticipated; the boats were ordered to be lowered.

"Then there was an ugly rush by some of the foreign male passengers to get first into the boats, and they had to be restrained by force, and the women and children given the first chance. These helpless creatures were hustled into a boat, and only two Lascar sailors with them, who were supposed to understand crossing the surf. It was now too dark to cross the reef, and if the night had been a rough one, every creature in the heavily-laden boats would have been drowned.

"After a terrible night of anxiety, bobbing about in the open boats, day began to dawn, and the attempt was made to land the people. The captain imagined that the jungle was full of wild beasts, but the danger from the sea was much greater. One boat made the rush, and was watched with the greatest anxiety. It got through all right, but was caught by a huge roller and upset before touching the shore. One poor lady was drowned ; the rest of the passengers managed to land. The other boats, by some miracle, did not lose any of their passengers.

"I was in the fourth boat myself, and we kept hovering round the ship all night, taking off a man at a time to transfer to one of the other boats. The danger of this proceeding was that, if we approached too near, four or five Lascars would jump on at once from the forearm and swamp us. The captain and pilot were the last to leave, and were taken out of the rigging.

"On landing, the first thing we did was to bury poor Mrs. Desinger. Her husband had a presentiment that she would be drowned on the voyage, and tried to make her give it up, even after she was on board, and he was saying good-bye to her at Calcutta. But she was going to the wedding of her only son, and would not be persuaded to remain. She was a most charming, pretty woman, and quite self-possessed in all the danger. I remember asking her if she had any one looking after her, and if she had saved anything out of her cabin, when she said No. I went down and fetched her hand-bag and some things. She told me calmly she was sure she would be drowned. When she was washed ashore she looked quite beautiful, with such a peaceful expression. We found a silver cross washed up, and fastened it with some wood to mark the grave.

"Then parties were formed to explore, and tried several bush paths in different directions, but they all ended nowhere; so it was decided to march along the coast. The sun soon dried our clothes, but some had lost their shoes, and we had to carry the women and children at all the worst places. It was broiling hot, and our feet and faces got fearfully blistered. We had lost all our head gear, and had to walk for three days in this manner, crossing many water-courses, the water often up to one's waist, subsisting on the milk of cocoa-nuts, and a little rice that we procured at some of the native huts.

"One poor lady had two little children of nine months and two years old. The passengers were a mixed lot—Italians, French, and Germans.

"I succeeded one day in getting a bottle of milk and some bread for the babies, who, with their mother, were far in the rear of the procession; but my feet were so blistered that I asked the native Sin-galese to take it to them, and, would you believe it, two horrid Frenchmen inter-cepted him and drank it up themselves.

"Trincomalee was the nearest port, and when we reached it at least sixty of us had to be sent to the Infirmary. The last few miles we procured some bullock carts for the women and children.

"Of course our plight was instantly

telegraphed, and a small steamer sent to convey us to Colombo.   It had only cabin accommodation for fifteen, and we were 150, so you may imagine we had an uncomfortable four days of it aboard her. All the men had to sleep on deck, and wet weather made it worse.   We lost every stitch of clothes, and everything we had with us.   My kodak floated ashore, and as I had done several photos : while the ship was sinking, I carried it with me, and have since had some of them developed, which were not too much spoilt by the sand."

This is the unvarnished narrative of this plucky young fellow ; he and his friend came from Cheshire, and seemed to have travelled a great deal.   All the children in the *Mariposa* were devoted to them, as they were so kind to the little ones.

On *Thursday, 6th April,* after much

rough weather, we reached Honolulu at sunset; but it was dark before we got into the harbour and were allowed to land. The beautiful green hills glowed in the evening light. We landed with Miss S—— (a charming lady who corresponds with one of the leading papers at home), Baron Luttwitz, Dr. Scheidel (a German), and Monsieur Perêt (a Russian), and went to the hotel.

The land felt so firm under one's feet after the deck, as we tramped through the streets, and saw shadowy palm-trees at every corner all round the hotel. The palms and bushes were festooned with electric lights, and an excellent Portuguese band played for some time.

What we liked best of all was a big packet of letters from home and newspapers, which it took us some time to read.

We then heard that the Island dancers, whom we had taken on board at Apia for the Chicago Exhibition, were going to give a performance in the theatre, so we all hurried off there and saw all the dances. It was very interesting, as they were all in their national costume.

One dance with war paddles was very wild indeed, and they clashed them together and shouted in time to the music, which consisted of tom-toms, also played by natives. They wore huge, white sort of turban helmets, stuck full of feathers, and those coloured belts I told you of—all tags of different shades; their long brown arms and legs flying about in all directions. No words can paint the strangeness of their attitudes and gestures. The only thing I have seen the least like it was a small sketch the Duke did in India of a devil dance.

We were tired before the end of the show, and returned to the hotel, where we made an excellent supper—the first I had really enjoyed for a long time! Round the walls of the dining-room were terrific pictures of the volcano Kaulauea and lake of fire. Baron Luttwitz remained in Honolulu on purpose to make the expedition. You have to go 200 miles, first in a small steamer, and ride the rest of the way, I believe.

Mr. Woodhouse, the English Consul, came to see me; the letters had all been sent to his care. As we had only landed to take in cargo, and were twenty hours late, and feared to miss the mail at San Francisco, the captain would not wait till daylight, and we were all on board again by twelve o'clock.

We had quite expected to come in for a revolution at Honolulu to reinstate the

Queen, who had so recently been deposed ; but we found the inhabitants taking it very coolly, and saying they were quite sure she would be reinstated by the English !

Three rough days followed this pleasing interlude on shore in the Sandwich Islands. One used to be woke up in the morning by the things banging about in the cabin, and my maid often landed on my knee when trying to dress me. We got a good many bruises, and one morning I put my foot into a glass of lemonade, in climbing out of my berth, but fortunately did not break the glass. One lived in a constant state of mess and discomfort. If one tried to write on deck the paper used to blow away, and one jumped up to rescue it, and upset the ink—a great crime—and had to send for the quarter-master to mop it up.

At last, on Monday, 10th, the sea began to calm down a little, and I was able to go down to the saloon for dinner. The obliging little stewardess had to bring me many meals on deck that voyage; she was such a pretty little American, with dark eyes and curly grey hair, and a very slight figure. She told us she was a grandmother, so I told her I had several grandchildren too, alas! only step-ones.

The calm only lasted a day; on Tuesday, 11th, the sea was up again, and head wind as strong as ever. Drenchings from big waves every now and then. It also became much colder, and we had to get out fur cloaks, and all the winter clothes we could lay our hands on.

On the evening of Thursday we entered the harbour of San Francisco by the Golden Gate, in the midst of a fine sunset. I must tell you that the harbour is sixty miles long, so we had not quite arrived till long after dark.

We were met by all sorts of people, who had been written to, to take care of us. Railway agent, manager of hotel, other people's friends, etc., and got quite bewildered when we found two sets of rooms had been engaged for us at different hotels.

After getting a small bag for the night and a few pieces of hand-baggage smuggled through the Custom-house, we at length, after tipping everybody all round, left the ship with glad hearts, and drove to the wonderful Palace Hotel.

Oh, how delightful it was to get into large comfortable beds, and eat supper at a steady table! No one who has not been a voyage can understand the joy of eating on shore again. People were so kind to us, and sent us heaps of the most lovely flowers : la France roses, Parma and white violets, scarlet carnations, and boxes of heliotrope, till our sitting-room looked like a garden.

Friday, 14*th*, we spent in going to the bank, post-office, and railway agent's (Mr. M'Kay) office, to arrange our trip across America, and take our sleeping-car tickets. In the evening we were asked to dine and go to the play with some friends.

On *Saturday*, 15*th*, Mr. T——— called for us in his buggy, with fast-trotting horses, and drove us out to a place called the Cliff House, all through the park, which is seven miles long. We lunched at the Cliff House, on oysters and terrabin (young turtle), etc. ; and from the veranda one looks down on a huge rock in the sea, called the Seals' Rock. It was covered with enormous seals, some of them all wet and glistening, just out of the water, others had been lying in the sun till they were quite dry, and their coats a bright yellow-brown colour.   It was the most extraordinary sight.

Our drive was really twelve miles long, but it only took about forty minutes with these fast horses.   It was like flying, and most enjoyable.

In the evening we asked our hospitable host to dine with us, and all went afterwards to see " China Town." First to the Chinese joss house, where there were a whole row of hideous Chinese idols, very small, with real hairy beards.   All the carving, and beautiful silk hangings, and banners, and rows of silver-headed spears, were most curious.   The keeper of the joss house allowed us to try our fortunes without bowing down to the idols, by shaking a long wooden spill out of a spill box from among a number of others, and hunting up the number of our respective spills in a Chinese fortune-book. He told me I should have very good luck in three months, and let us hope he meant we should get safe home; but we won't take three months about it.

We then proceeded to the Chinese theatre, where foreigners are only allowed to sit on chairs on the stage at the sides. The dresses worn by the actors were most gorgeous, all embroidered with gold, and made of red, yellow, and blue silk. I attempted some sketches, but in that noise and heat, with inquisitive Chinese looking over one's shoulder and laughing, it was no easy matter. No Chinese woman is allowed to act on a public stage, so their parts are taken by men, and a good actor of women's parts earns a very high salary, especially if he has a squeaky voice.

The piece was evidently extremely

amusing to the Chinese audience, who were packed as tight as herring in a barrel, and all standing; the few women and girls present were seated in a balcony.

The story, as translated to us, was of the Enoch Arden style. The husband returns from a long absence to find his wife in bridal attire, marrying another man. The rival husbands fight a duel on the stage with spears, and they were so close to us, that we expected every moment at least to lose our hats in the wild twirling of swords and other weapons that ensued.

After remaining nearly an hour, and seeing a variety of gorgeous costumes, we took our departure by the back of the stage, through all the actors, who crowded round, asking to see the sketches we had done. We heard they were not over pleased, as they thought, perhaps, we were doing them for the police!

The entrance to the theatre by the back way is through a labyrinth of filthy dark passages, with little ladders for stairs. If the building chanced to take fire every one would be suffocated like rats in a trap. We were then conducted to see some opium dens, where the devotees of that noxious herb were enjoying themselves, smoking pipes of it on fine mats, with a little lamp beside them to melt the balls of opium before stuffing it into their pipes. By this time we were tired and thirsty, and delighted to mount the stairs of a Chinese tea-house, where some delicious green tea was served in covered cups, with a lot of little plates of ginger, cake, and sweetmeats.

The room was very quaint, full of beautiful lacquered carving and round tables; and a sort of dais, where the Chinamen sit when they have a party of friends and dancing-girls perform for them.

We had walked altogether about three hours in China Town, and it was nearly twelve o'clock when we got home. We bought a few trifles at a Chinese shop as remembrances of the expedition.

There was a charming collection of miniatures being exhibited at our hotel, which we went to see. Several of Napoleon Buonaparte and Josephine, and Marie Louise and her son, the little king of Rome ; and also some lovely Cosways of ladies in powdered hair.

On *Sunday*, 16*th*, we both had rather bad colds after our nocturnal rambles, and nursed them up all morning. In the afternoon we returned several calls, and saw two beautiful houses full of wonderful furniture and pictures. The town of San Francisco is most picturesquely situated, all up and down hill, with beautiful views of the sea and hills at every turn. It reminded us a little of Edinburgh, some of the streets are so steep.

Next morning we left this hospitable city at 7.30, having the good luck to secure a drawing-room private car on the railroad, which we inhabited till Tuesday evening, when we reached Salt Lake City. We were waited on by the negro car porter in blue uniform. He made our berths for us in the evening with plenty of clean sheets and pillows ; most comfortable they were, and very soundly we slept in them—in fact, rather too soundly, as by the time we were dressed it was nearly twelve o'clock, and the black cook informed us we would have to have lunch, as breakfast was over long ago. I believe, in the public sleeping-car, people get up from six to eight in the morning.

They bring your meals in on a tray, and fix up a little sliding table to serve them on, which is also very convenient for writing or painting. We did some rapid sketches of the scenery as we went along, and we stopped at a great many stations. Soon after leaving Sacramento City the grass began to get a vivid green, and the prairie was carpeted with masses of violet and yellow flowers. The large yellow buttercup is the flower of California. As the railroad ascended into the Rocky Mountains the air got keener, and the flowers ceased. Beautiful snowy ranges of mountains succeeded each other. The ranches were very bare of grass, and several skeletons of cattle were seen.

At one place we passed a tribe of Indians on the move; they were mounted on horses, and dressed in every variety of gaudy garments, with feather head-dresses.

Strange to say, we were not very tired when we reached Salt Lake City, the air was so wonderful and exhilarating. Hilda enjoyed some snowballing with a fellow-passenger.

On *Wednesday, 19th*, we hired a landau, and proceeded to make a tour of the city. There is a magnificent view from the Fort, about three miles distant, where the soldiers' barracks and officers' houses are. You see Salt Lake in the far distance; it is called the Dead Sea by the Mormons, and a river, called the Jordan, runs between it and a smaller lake, which they call the Sea of Galilee. Salt Lake is about seventy miles long. The plains extend for many miles, and are bounded by the snow-capped peaks of the Rockies, which rise to a great height just outside the town.

We saw the soldiers drilling, and one

company that is composed of Indians — fine-looking fellows in blue uniforms, with Tyrolese fawn-coloured hats. Our driver told us various Mormon tales, and pointed out Brigham Young's former houses, where he stowed his numerous wives.

A law has been passed of late years forbidding the Latter-Day Saints a plurality of spouses, so the rising generation have to content themselves with one wife apiece. Brigham Young had thirty-six wives and forty-seven children, and I don't know how many grandchildren. Every one who is not a Mormon is called a Gentile in Salt Lake City. I did an oil sketch from the windows of the hotel, which shows the old inn in the foreground. One of the reporters from the *Salt Lake Herald* called, and I had to give him an interview while painting it, as the sun was going down rapidly. He made a paragraph of the interview, which amused us very much.

On *Thursday, 20th*, left our splendid hotel at Salt Lake with much regret, as it was so comfortable. Started at 8 A.M., and failing to get a drawing-room car or even a section for that day, were just going to sit in the public car with some cowboys, when a kind couple took pity on us, and offered us seats in their section till the evening, when we secured a car for ourselves.

The views that day were grander and grander. We lunched at a place a little beyond Castle Gate, a huge rampart of red sandstone. In fact, it was difficult to realise that all the walls, and fortresses, and castles we saw were not the work of human hands. The line went through a succession of cañons, with rivers flowing between the rocky ramparts. We passed numerous cattle ranches, and saw some red deer towards evening on the bank of the river.

The negro cook in our compartment told several thrilling tales of murders, and pointed out the graves of three cowboys who had been shot by a rancher for stealing his cattle. The latter calmly wired for three coffins to be sent down next morning, in which he buried them. He had of course to stand his trial, but was let off, people in these wild parts having a strong feeling for summary justice.

We enjoyed this journey enormously, and sat at the end of the train eating Florida oranges and dust, and looking at each lovely scene as we sped along.

We reached Colorado Springs at 5.30 on Friday morning (April 21st), and

had to turn out of our warm beds.
Only one room could we procure, and
had to wait two hours for it in a cold
parlour, where we fell asleep on sofas till
the housemaid began to brush and sweep
round us. It was an uncomfortable arrival;
but after hot baths and breakfast we felt
better, and sallied forth in a buggy to see
some of the wonders of that most wonderful place.

We had two charming cream-coloured
ponies, with long tails. The Americans
have the greatest contempt for " dock -
tailed horses," as they call the English
ones. We drove to the " Garden of the
Gods." It is a tract of country where
there are extraordinary formations of
red sandstone in every conceivable shape.
Walls of fiery red form the gateway to this enchanted place, and beyond
you see the snowy summit of Pike's Peak,

a mountain nearly as high as Mont Blanc. The different forms these rocks take are very eccentric : for instance, there is the

MONUMENT PARK.

bear and the lamb kissing each other ; a figure of a man with a periwig, in robes of state ; frogs, lizards, the Queen, the Siamese Twins, the Cook's Cap, etc., etc.

—all natural, and owing nothing to art. We stopped at a small hostelry, on the window of which was written in gold letters, *Stop and see the Fat Man.* Out he came, as large as life, and provided us with milk, bread and cheese, and a great deal of amusing conversation. We bought photos from him, and I sat a long time in the veranda doing a sketch of the gateway and Pike's Peak.

Saturday, 22nd.—My sister's wedding day. Alas! that we were not home in time to assist at the ceremony. We sent a cablegram with loving congratulations, and spent the day having a delightful picnic at the Cheyenne Cañon, an even more lovely spot than any we had previously visited. Enormous red cliffs, clothed at their base with pine and silver fir. A waterfall in the south cañon, with seven falls, and snow peaks beyond. I saw a little animal that I took for a prairie dog, but afterwards discovered that it was called a Tasmanian devil. It was striped like a tiger, and had a pointed nose. The middle of its body was orange colour, and it had a small bushy tail like a squirrel, which it rather resembled. We also noticed several lovely blue birds and prairie larks with yellow breasts.

Sunday, 23rd April. — Went to the Episcopal church, and heard beautiful singing. Drove in our spider buggy, with the chestnut pony, in the afternoon to the Utah Pass by a winding road up the mountain. We reached the Great Caverns, and were shown through them by the guide, armed with lamps, as it was pitch dark inside. They were only discovered in 1885 by the whites, although known to the red men. We saw one skull and cross-bones of an Indian, and his necklace of beads that had been found there.

We met an Englishman at the Caverns, Mr. Heber Percy, who was delighted to talk what he called English with us, as he had been travelling alone, and had heard nothing but American !

We were equally pleased to hear news of many English friends, as he had come straight out from home. He was surprised to find that my grand-aunt had married his grand-uncle ; but that is always the way when you come to investigate—every stranger you meet almost has some connecting link. I had also known his sister in former days.

We heard a most wonderful instrument played in the Caverns ; it was a musical set of stalactites, like the pipes of an organ, and the melody was produced by hitting them with a small stick. It had only been discovered about four years ago by the man who played to us on it.

PIKE'S PEAK, FROM THE GARDEN OF THE GODS.

We left Colorado Springs on Tuesday, 25th, at 10.40, having spent Monday again sketching the stupendous' scenery at the "Garden of the Gods." It was only a three hours' journey to Denver City. We had rooms at the Brown Palace Hotel, the speculation of a millionaire, and vastly successful—a wonder of good taste and comfort. The lifts make one quite giddy ; they rush you up and down at such a pace.

On *Wednesday, 26th*, we made the tour of the city, Mr. Howard, the helpful railway agent, having procured us a charming little open carriage, a sort of cross between a pony phaeton and a Victoria, with a pair of dashing white horses. Almost every street is full of handsome buildings, and bordered by trees ; in another month they will be out, but these towns are so high that spring is late, and rain much wanted at present. The villas keep their lawns green by constant watering. Six hundred miles of prairie stretch away from the city ; 300 miles are fertile, and much is being done in the way of irrigation, which causes " the desert to rejoice and blossom as the rose." If you are not all tired of reading this epistle, I am of writing it, so adieu for the present.

P.S.—We propose to sail for England on the 17th May in the *Majestic.*

BALANCE ROCK, GARDEN OF THE GODS.

NIAGARA.

LETTER No. 11.

RICHELIEU HOTEL,
CHICAGO, *Friday, 28th April* 1893.

WE left Denver City at 9 A.M., and jour-
neyed over the 600 miles of arid, yellow
plains.   Several times the engine grunted,
and some unfortunate bullock was tossed
off the line by the cow-catcher, and left
to die, with its back broken, at the foot
of the embankment.

The dust and heat were intolerable ; we

slept in the drawing-room car that night. On the whole, we have become so satiated with magnificent scenery, that we found it quite a relief to read a book and not look out of windows.

About thirty miles from Chicago we were met by Mr. Wilson, another of those obliging station agents who make things so smooth for unprotected females in America. He brought us our letters, and about 5 P.M. we reached Chicago, and drove to the Richelieu Hotel, where we secured some rooms lately occupied by Adelina Patti, and supposed to be very luxurious — all opening into each other with folding doors, and beds that hooked themselves up into mirrored wardrobes, the walls hung with good modern pictures, and thick pile carpets on the floors: they were well situated, over-looking the street and the steamboat pier, with Lake Michigan as a back ground.

Next morning, *Saturday*, *29th*, we saw detachments of troops pass, both cavalry and infantry, escorting the Duke of Veragua and the President in open carriages from the station. Then there was the procession of the Bell of Liberty. It was drawn along by thirteen horses on a car, with a live eagle, who looked extremely uncomfortable perched on some laurels at the top, followed by mounted police. This was the first bell sounded after the War of Independence was over.

Fine weather, but cold and raw. We were called on by General and Mrs. M'Clurg and Mr. M'Cormick, who took us to an art gallery where there was a fine collection of old pictures. It was being opened in connection with the Exhibition, and was still full of workmen unpacking statuary.

On *Sunday*, 20*th*, Mrs. M'Clurg fetched us in her carriage, and we went to service at St. James's Church—a very large, handsome edifice.

Monday, 1*st May*, was the great day of the opening ceremony at the World's Columbian Exhibition. Our kind friends had secured excellent places for us, very near the President, where we could hear his speech ; and one of them, Mr. Aldis, came to escort us to the station, where we entered the special train, with a lot of dignitaries, and were introduced to several charming American ladies.

Comparatively few of the fair sex in Chicago honoured this festive ceremony with their presence, as the day was so threatening, and the mud we had to wade through to reach the building was so deep! Also many of them were reserving themselves for the opening of the Women's Section later in the day. We were glad that we had not been dissuaded from taking part in the big function, for the impressive scene will remain fixed in our memories for ever.

When the President declared the Exhibition open, and touched the electric spring which set the whole thing in motion, the effect was extremely thrilling. Round and round the magnificent buildings the flags of every nation flew up to the tops of the flagstaffs, while every boat and gondola on the lake rushed from its hiding-place, gaily decorated with bunting; and the veils which enveloped the colossal golden statue of Liberty slowly fell off.

The whole area in front of the chief building was a mass of humanity, and as they kept crowding from all points towards the middle to hear the President's speech, many adventurous females in the crowd began to get squashed. Naturally some shrieking ensued, and a good many limp forms were extracted from the throng and perched on the packing-cases, where the cameras of a swarm of photographers were stationed.

At one time it was feared the mob would try to rush the barriers, and break in amongst us; but some extra police were called up, and order restored.

That afternoon my cousin, the Master of Elibank, arrived, having crossed in the *Campania.* You may imagine what a pleasure it was to see some one fresh from England, and hear all the home news, and also to have some one to dine with us and control the waiters, half of whom had gone off on strike to the Exhibition, leaving the hotel proprietor tearing his hair and obliged to hire a scratch

pack, who were the reverse of brilliant.
The first night we had dined in a comfortable room up stairs, with shaded lamps and
everything nicely done; but after that a
restaurant was opened on the ground
floor, which was both hot and noisy, and
glaring with electric light. All sorts of
people used to come in from other hotels,
in most fantastic costume, and after the
strike we simply had to wait about two
hours for the smallest dinner. The servants were worse off, as they could hardly
get anything to eat at all.

Who should turn up one day but my
butler, whom I had placed in a temporary
situation before leaving England, and who
was travelling with his master as valet,—
certainly the last person one expected to
appear in Chicago and offer to do one's
messages.

On *Tuesday, 2nd May*, Mr. M'Cormick

lionised us indefatigable tourists all round the town. We insisted on going to see the Panorama of the Great Fire—perfectly fearful it must have been from the rapidity with which it spread. Multitudes of people were pursued by the flames to the shore of Lake Michigan, and had to wade into the water and stand in it all night.

We were also taken to the top of the Tower of the Auditorium in a lift, from whence there was a bird's-eye view of the city; very fine and most interesting to have pointed out to us on the real live map the different points where the fire began and spread to.

We afterwards drove round Lincoln Park and by the esplanade on the shore of the lake, and saw the fine statues of Lincoln and Grant.

Wednesday, 3rd, we spent again at the

Exhibition; saw the Buildings of Agriculture and Manufactures, and the Art Building with the splendid collections of pictures in the British. German, and Austrian sections. No words can say how much we admired them, or how hungry we were when lunch time arrived! Alas! there wasn't time to see the French gallery.

As there are 400 miles of walks and corridors to disport yourself in at this great show, it used to make me full of rage to hear people say that there was not enough finished for them to see, and that the place was in a mess and full of packing-cases. The papers took up the same tune, and really did a great deal of harm by preventing lots of people coming who would have liked to see it early in the season before the great rush, but were quite put off it by all this stupid twaddle.

I thought it a very sensible plan that so many schools gave the pupils a sort of course of the Exhibition, as they would learn so much more in a short space than books could teach.

We were particularly fascinated by the lovely collections of stuffed birds; and there were some cases of life-sized models of different Indian tribes in beautiful deerskin dresses, dyed yellow and pale green—even the children's dresses quite complete. Also specimens of their bead-work in all the loveliest shades, hunting pouches, mocassins, papoose cradles, etc., etc. Then the Mexican Indians made most elaborate and gorgeous feather dresses, all from the plumage of brilliant small birds, parrots, etc.

Very near the Indians were some interesting models of war-ships and passenger steamers; a model of Mr. Burdett Coutts's

Brookfield stud also attracted our attention.

We paid a hasty visit to the Women's
Section, but had not really time to see the
lace and other lovely things, as we had to
return to Chicago in time to dress for Mrs.
Potter Palmer's reception in the afternoon.
I bought a lovely French bonnet for the
occasion, trimmed with violets and a little
pink rose. General M'Clurg called to fetch
me in his brougham, and on the way he
showed me his book-store, full of such
fascinating editions that it was hard to
tear one's self away. After serving most
gallantly in the war he turned printer, and
does a great business in books. The day
I left he sent me some charming little
volumes for a remembrance of my visit to
Chicago, although we did not require anything to remind us of the great kindness
and hospitality we received there.

At Mrs. Palmer's reception swarms and swarms of people were introduced, and I was delighted with the bright way they entered at once into conversation and made one feel at home. The Duchess of Veragua and her daughter were there, and Lord and Lady Aberdeen, and so many pretty faces and smart frocks, wonderful furniture, hangings, and costly pictures. The whole thing was most bewildering, and like a brilliant dream.

That evening we dined with General and Mrs. M'Clurg at their beautiful home. The chimney-piece in the library is all carved with military trophies, and the names of the various battles in which the General took part—a delightful heirloom for his son.

Afterwards we joined the Duke and Duchess of Veragua at the play: a spectacular piece, with a ballet and processions of all the different states and nations and their trains in wonderful costumes. All were asked on to supper afterwards at a club. Certainly that day we didn't let the grass grow under our feet, and were pretty well tired out when we got to bed.

Next morning, *Thursday, May 4th*, we were asked to go a coaching expedition of the Four-in-hand Club with the Veraguas and all the "society"; but, alas! we were obliged to content ourselves with seeing the teams start in brilliant sunshine, with many regrets that we were unable to join them.

Our train for Niagara left at 5 P.M., and we arrived at the Falls at 7.30 on Friday morning.

We only secured sleeping berths in the public car, and I lost a beloved diamond brooch in the shape of a bee, which was very vexing, as it was a wedding present from an old friend. At the first view of the Falls the train stops for five minutes, and everybody, at least all who are dressed, bundle out to see them.

The day was rather cold and dull, so we thought a good walk would be beneficial. Alick,[1] Hilda, and I sallied forth after dressing and breakfast at the hotel, and made a tour of the islands; got covered with spray at Horse Shoe Fall, then walked on to the Rapids above the Falls, and sat watching the foaming, fascinating green waters for a long time.

After lunch we drove four miles on a most atrocious road to the Whirlpool and Rapids, and saw the place where poor Webb was drowned. Every one has heard so much of the Falls that I must not launch forth on the subject of their grandeur and

[1] The Master of Elibank.

beauty. Later in the summer, when all the cotton trees are in spring garments, it must be lovely ; as it was, the grass was carpeted with wild flowers, and, fortunately, there are notices up to prevent ruthless tourists from tearing them up by handfuls. Before leaving we invested in some Indian dollies for my "*grandchildren !*" I attempted one or two tiny sketches.

We started for New York at 5.30 ; had a smart drawing-room car, and slept like ten tops. Arrived at 8 A.M., and drove to Holland House. After baths and breakfast sallied forth in search of clothes, and each found a decent reach-me-down suit for our homeward voyage.

On Sunday we were rather late for church, so turned in at the small church of the Transfiguration, which, to our surprise, seemed to be full of white veiled figures in the centre aisle. It turned out that a confirmation service was going to be held. As the light from the stained glass windows was very "dim and religious," it made quite a pretty and mysterious scene, and worthy the brush of a skilful artist.

On *Tuesday*, *9th*, we went with friends to visit some of the men-of-war then anchored in the Hudson. Had tea out of a samovar on board the Russian flag-ship *Demitri Douskoi*, whose officers were most hospitable, and showed us everything. We also boarded the American flag-ship *Chicago*, and had much interesting conversation with Captain Sperry.

We paid a visit to the Zoo and Central Park, where all the trees were bursting into leaf. The weather was very hot and trying, and we were glad to get out of town, after a sad farewell to Alick, who sailed for Antigua.

On *Wednesday, 10th*, crossed the Ferry, and took the train to Philadelphia, where we were the guests of Mr. George Childs, who came to meet us at the station and take us on in the local train to Bryn Maur, where his carriages met us; we had a lovely drive through a fertile country, with many fruit-trees in blossom, and the greenest of green grass. Passed many dainty villas and country homes, and eventually drove up an approach, through well-kept, smooth-shaven turf, to Wootton House, so named by Mr. and Mrs. Childs after our Wotton in Buckinghamshire, but spelt differently to insure its proper pronunciation. Such a pretty red brick house, with deep veranda.

That evening there was a large dinner party. I sat next Dr. da Costa, and found he had known the Duke, and been at Stowe in former days. Mr. Frank Thomson (Vice-President of the Pennsylvanian Railroad) and his pretty daughter were also of the party. He very kindly offered us his private car for our journey to Washington. We were delighted to accept, as it was the wish of our hearts to travel in one.

Thursday, 11*th*, I was taken to see the Ladies' College for the higher education of women. We were received by the (female) dean, and shown all over the buildings. It was quite a journey through it. Swarms of "girl graduates" in cap and gown. I begged for a photo of one of them, and a very pretty " freshman's " was afterwards sent me.

Various young professors were engaged in giving lectures on a variety of abstruse subjects. We peeped into the lecture rooms, opening the swing doors very carefully, and I considered the climax of research was reached when we found on the top story a laboratory, where a plaster cast of a man's brains had just been successfully executed. The professor in charge of the brain, which was still on a plate, said, "the fellow who once owned it was doing more good now than he had ever done in life"; so we supposed it was the brain of a criminal, or a very frivolous person.

On our return there was a large luncheon party of eighteen ladies, which lasted three hours, after which I planted a tree on the lawn, and we visited the farm and greenhouses.

Some more friends were invited to dinner, but, alas! I was suddenly seized with a touch of influenza—the "grip," as they call it here—and had to retire from the fray and go to bed.

Next morning we were to have started

at eight, to go and lionise in Philadelphia, and see the "Drexel Institute" and the "Ledger Office," both creations of Mr. Childs, but I felt too ill for such an early start, so Hilda went with Mr. Childs, and I joined by a train which left at eleven o'clock. Our kind host and hostess, and Miss Thomson, saw us off in her father's luxurious car, with two negro servants to cook and wait on us.

We arrived at Washington about four o'clock, and were met at the station by Sir Julian Pauncefote, who drove us to the Embassy, where Lady Pauncefote and her daughters welcomed us most hospitably, and we had a time of real rest and refreshment, while we stayed in their delightful house.

I was most anxious to see the views of the city and everything that was to be seen, so, in spite of my influenza, I went

SIR JULIAN PAUNCEFOTE, G.C.B.

To face p.

about, and they took us some beautiful drives. The finest view was from Arlington, the military cemetery, which used to be General Lee's country seat.

A pleasant episode was my visit to the White House, where Mrs. Cleveland, the President's pretty young wife, very kindly gave me an audience.

Hilda happened to go one day with Miss Duncombe to see the state-rooms, and hearing the President was just holding his weekly reception, at which any one has the right to attend, they went in and shook hands with him. He was amused to see Miss Duncombe, who explained who Hilda was, and how they came to be at " The White House " on a reception day.

One evening Mr. Boucher was one of the guests at dinner, and we went afterwards to see his Company act in " Twelfth Night " at the National Theatre.

This delightful visit was only too soon over, and on Wednesday, 17th May, we had to say good-bye to them all, and start for New York.   Dined with some friends in Fifth Avenue, and went on board the *Majestic* after dinner.   It is a splendid liner and no mistake.   One didn't mind the rolling on such a large scale, and we had one of the best three berth-cabins, and were more than comfortable.

Canon Leigh (a brother of Lady Jersey's) and his wife and daughter were among the passengers, and plenty of other nice people, but the weather was too cold to make many acquaintances, and after the other long voyages the time passed very quickly, beguiled by quails and other good things, not forgetting the contents of two large *bonbonnières* which we found in our state-room.

There was a most attractive library on

INDIAN SCOUT.

From a Sketch by Craig.)

board, every sort of interesting book, and little writing-tables and comfortable arm-chairs, and a *most* comfortable stewardess.

On Tuesday, 23rd, we got some letters at Queenstown, and reached Liverpool at 6.30 on Wednesday morning, 24th.   A great display of bunting in the harbour, *not* for our arrival, but for the Queen's birthday.   After our colonial and guber-natorial experiences, we quite felt that it might be for us.

Thus ended our tour.   Unlike most travellers, our pleasure in getting home was mingled with deep regret that it was all over, and that my cabin mate and I must now go different ways and dissolve partnership.

INDEX

THE END

Printed by R. & R. Clark, *Edinburgh*